# MAKE ME SMILE

## Bayshore #6

# Ember Leigh

Published by Ember Leigh, 2021

EmberLeighAuthor@gmail.com

Cover art: Covers by Combs

Editing: Elisabeth R. Nelson

# ABOUT 'MAKE ME SMILE'

**I never imagined I'd be a graceful bride.**

I stained my wedding dress the second I tried it on. Connor even accidentally saw it in my camera roll. And worst yet? Our parents would rather attend our wedding via Zoom than spend an entire evening rubbing elbows with their arch nemeses.

Three years into our HEA and things just keep getting better, except for this one little nagging area of our life. I want our marriage to form a truce between the Dalys and Cabanas, but with us living so far away from Bayshore, all we've been able to accomplish is a resentful stalemate.

But now that Connor and I are back in Bayshore for our extended wedding-and-beyond home-cation, our to-do list includes not just finalizing floral arrangements, but also getting our Moms and Dads to bury the hatchet.

Cocktail parties with ex-best friends? Check. Fishing trips with two frosty fathers? Agonizing check.

Connor and I are determined to forge a new future for our parents, no matter how much we grimace through it.

But on my wedding day, there's no doubt about it. This man—and this life we've built—will do nothing but make me smile.

# CHAPTER ONE

KINSLEY

"Good god, woman." Connor lets out an exaggerated groan as he hoists my wheeled luggage out of the trunk of the ride share. He acts like it weighs a million pounds, but I know it doesn't. It probably weighs fifty-five, if I know my luggage-packing habits.

But the groan doesn't fool me. He enjoys it. I can see it in the smile tugging at the corner of his lips as he lowers the lid of the trunk.

"I thought you were used to me packing fifty books per trip by now," I tell him sweetly as the ride share driver peers at us through the rear-view mirror. "This is our, what, sixth trip together to Bayshore? Your biceps should know what to expect."

"Oh, trust me," Connor says with a grin as he taps the back of the car. The driver nods and pulls away, leaving us lost in each other's gaze in front of Door 3 at the San Diego Airport Departures area. "My biceps are ready for this suitcase and everything else that's waiting for us."

"Oh yeah?"

"Up to and including all the shower sex," he says in a low voice, his hot breath brushing my ear lobe. A shiver goes down my spine, and I erupt into giggles as he nips at my earlobe. A car honks behind us—we've been canoodling on the road for long enough. Connor sweeps his arm around my waist and guides us onto the sidewalk, tugging our luggage behind us.

"I just would like to make it known," I go on as we head for the sliding doors of the airport entrance, "that my books are not the *only* reason my luggage is heavy this time."

"Sunny-kins, your luggage could weigh three hundred pounds and I'd gladly lift it, *and* pay the overweight fee," he says.

"Awww." A big grin breaks out on my face, one that I'm incapable of controlling. My cheeks are hurting in no time. "See? That's why I'm marrying you. Because you say sweet shit like that."

He laughs, keeping his arm around my waist as we stride into the gleaming airport. We've taken this trip back home enough times as a couple now to have the route down—the most recent time just last month, for London and Dom's wedding. But this time, it's different. Because we're entering as boyfriend and girlfriend, but we'll be returning to this airport as Mr. and Mrs. Daly.

And I could not be more excited.

"Hopefully that's not the *only* reason you're marrying me," he says with a sidelong glance.

"That, and your biceps. And the fact that you allow me to remain the undisputed ping-pong champion of the relationship, despite the clear threat to your masculinity."

He breaks into laughter as we roll up to the check-in desk. There's not much of a crowd today, for some reason, so we're waited on almost instantly. When the airline clerk asks for my name, I'm still thinking about the fact that I'll be returning to this airport a married woman.

"Kinsley Connor," I blurt, and then pause. "I mean, Kinsley Daly. I'm—" A sigh escapes me as Connor hides his laughter behind his closed fist. "Let me try this again. Kinsley Cabana. We have the two o'clock flight to Cleveland."

The clerk lifts a brow, which I take as an invitation to continue supplying information.

"We're getting married," I tell her. "In just under a week."

"Congratulations," she says, sending me a genuine smile. To Connor, she says, "And you must be the Connor Daly on this reservation. I need your IDs please."

She prints our boarding passes while Connor and I share conspiratorial smiles. When it comes time for the luggage, his hits the mark, and I'm over by five pounds. *Nailed it.* He passes over the credit card wordlessly, and I just lace my fingers through his.

Once our luggage has disappeared down the conveyor belt, we're free to go through security. Connor and I walk hand-in-hand as though the welcome hall of the San Diego airport is as romantic as the Crystal Pier during a spectacular sunset. And hell, it sort of is. When this blond hunk is at my side, he turns everyday into a romantic adventure. Even three years into our relationship, we've only gotten a foot into the honeymoon phase.

"So, you really think Jaric and the crew will be able to handle us being gone for a month?" Connor is voicing the near-constant fear that we've been discussing for weeks. This is the first time we've ever truly stepped away from our brainchild, barring the one- or two-week visits to Bayshore each summer. But this time, we're not just taking a vacay. We're getting married, then going off the grid for a two-stop honeymoon in Aruba and the Dominican Republic, and *then* returning to Bayshore for one last family visit. And though we swore to be mostly unavailable for the duration of our wedding weekend and the honeymoon itself, we both know we'll be checking work emails daily.

"I think they will do an excellent job of handling any small fires that pop up," I tell him, which is the same mantra I've been using on myself for weeks now. "If there's anything big, we're always a phone call away."

"You're right." He squeezes my hand.

"And we need the time off," I remind him, even though I'm just as worried about things falling apart while we're gone. "We've been working like crazy to grow the business the past few years. Well, it's grown, and we need to celebrate."

"And we are going to fucking *celebrate*." He kisses my forehead as we approach security. The carry-on luggage checks go quickly, and soon we're strolling through Terminal 1 on our way to Gate 8.

"Speaking of which…" I dig my phone out from my purse, which is another so-ugly-it's-cute thrift find I picked up last month: a pink leather bag with parrots sewn into the side. "Hazel was supposed to send me the itinerary for this week."

"The itinerary?" Connor asks.

I swat his arm. "The pre-wedding itinerary! I told you about this."

"We're having a rehearsal on Friday…" he begins.

"Hazel mentioned that we could have a series of events leading up to the rehearsal for incoming guests and, well, the families in general." I swipe through screens, heading for our email thread. Hazel is my unofficial wedding planner, a role she volunteered for now that she and Grayson are happily married. Besides, I think she could see the fear in my eyes when we talked about wedding planning details a couple years back. She's the only one I would trust with managing such an important event. Hazel knows best—in realty *and* happily-ever-afters.

"Ummm," Connor begins, which tells me he did *not* hear me that evening I told him all about Hazel's plan for pre-wedding activities.

I sigh. "You and your selective hearing." I pull up the thread, finding a new email waiting for me. "Oh! She's just written back to confirm..." I scan the details quickly, my steps slowing until I'm stopped completely. Connor looks back at me.

"What's wrong?"

"Nothing, it's just..." I re-read her email, making sure I'm seeing correctly. Connor guides me off to the side of the thoroughfare. "We had been planning a series of activities, and I'm not gonna lie, I kinda told her to go warm fuzzy family on the planning."

"Okay..."

"And, well, she did exactly as she was told. But now that I'm seeing it..." I scan the list of events. Tuesday: cocktail party at our rental house for both families. Wednesday: fishing trip for fathers of the bride and groom. Thursday: final dress fitting. Friday: pedicures with the mothers, followed by rehearsal.

"Maybe this is too much," I say, shoving my phone into his hand so he could see the email. Hazel ended the email with an earnest question: *Are you sure this looks okay?*

No. I'm not sure of any of it now. This itinerary, which seemed so good in theory, is now poised to bring our parents together nearly every day in a seven-day period. Our parents, who barely tolerate the offspring of their rivals. Our parents, who were once best friends but have been blistering enemies for three decades.

Connor grimaces while he reads the email. "It looks fun."

"Then why does it look like you're getting a colonoscopy as you read it?"

He frowns, handing the phone back to me. "And this was your idea?"

"Yes! I want this to be the best wedding of our lives. Because it's *our* wedding. And, I don't know, I thought maybe we could finally start a new chapter with our families. Part of me thinks our parents have just been secretly hoping for the past three years that we'd end things and go our separate ways. Now we're getting married. I want this shit to be done with."

"I do too," Connor admits, placing his hand on my waist. "I think they're capable of it."

"They are. They've gone too long festering in this weird mountain of grudges," I go on, remembering the motivation I had when I asked Hazel to build the itinerary in the first place. "I'm sick of having to enter their caves like some sort of timid spelunker."

Connor furrows his brow. "They have caves...?"

"I want us all to live in harmony on the mountainside," I clarify. "They've spent thirty years cowering in their dark recesses of outrage and animosity. I'm sick of needing a headlamp to visit them."

"Ahh, yeah, the caves," Connor says. "We're gonna spelunk them into some goddamn family happiness."

"Right," I say, encouraged by his reaction. One of many reasons that I love this man: he at least pretends that my metaphors make sense to him. "Is that so bad? These activities are completely normal for any regular set of parents. I don't want to keep walking on eggshells when it comes to this. I'm the damn bride—aren't I supposed to call the shots?"

"You call all the shots," Connor affirms, "with or without headlamps."

I laugh, burying my face in his chest. "Thank you for that. So is it insane if we go ahead with this itinerary?"

"Not insane," he tells me, kissing the top of my head. "Dangerous, maybe. But what's the worst that could happen? This is our wedding, and we deserve to celebrate it as we choose."

I smile up at him, because he's right. What *is* the worst that can happen?

It's time to formally put this shit behind our collective families in the name of love...beginning Tuesday.

# CHAPTER TWO

CONNOR

Later that evening, Kinsley and I roll into Bayshore in our rental car—excuse me, rental *van*. Yes, the mid-sized sedan we reserved was inexplicably unavailable, leaving the only option at the Cleveland airport a maroon van capable of carrying a family of ten.

It's fine though. We're all smiles as we see the familiar sights through the windows of our family van—Hazel's realty billboard on Route 2 headed west, the maple tree-lined avenues that become more common the closer you get to the lake, and the humid tang in the air that is at once so similar to yet so different from San Diego.

"I cannot *wait* until we see our rental," Kinsley gushes suddenly. We booked a lakefront house for the duration of our stay. Partially to cling to whatever shreds of sanity we might need during the wedding week, but also because the thought of sharing a house with either set of parents just seems wrong. One family might feel like they were being preferred, and that's too many emotions to handle for a week like this. Nor would we want to uproot midway through the stay to switch houses just so we could say we stayed at each family's house equally—which is something else we actually considered.

No, the clear winner in this is the lakefront getaway. Jacuzzi patio included.

"What's the address again?" I ask as I turn the maroon behemoth onto Main Street. We wanted to wander Bayshore a bit first, which means I'm not even sure where we'll be staying.

"Oh, right. Hang on." Kinsley rummages through her purse to pull out her phone. She tuts when she assesses the screen. "Wait, this is your phone." She hands it off to me. We recently got a phone upgrade, but the two-for-one deal included the exact same style of phone—which has proved confusing every single day since. "Okay, here's mine. I think." She double checks the phone she handed back to me. It doesn't help that we even chose the same background image—a selfie we took at the office recently. "Yeah. This is mine. Okay, I still had it in airplane mode."

"Blessed silence."

She fiddles with the phone for a moment as I keep turning streets, enjoying the downtown scenes: the nineteenth-century architecture now inhabited by coffee shops and vintage stores; the sidewalks lined with potted plants; the quaint signs pointing toward historic sites. A series of *dings* and notifications buzz at her phone, catching up after airplane mode.

"Oh shit," she says.

"What is it?" My stomach clenches with anticipation, fearing the worst on the work front. I feel like both of us are just *waiting* for some big implosion to occur while we're gone.

"The rental house," she says slowly, brows furrowing as she reads. "They messaged me...and called me. But I missed them. Apparently the house isn't ready today."

I blink a few times, letting this news wash over me. My first thought is: *So the business is fine. Good.* Immediately followed by: *Wait, so what the fuck now?*

"Okay..." I begin.

Kinsley crumples a little, turning to me. "I'm going to call her back. She wrote that they could still honor our reservation. It'll just begin a little later."

"And what about the money we spent?" I ask.

"I'll find out." Kinsley swipes to call, pressing the phone to her ear as she stares out the window. I've brought us to the pier downtown, where parking lots look out over the choppy waters of Briggs Bay. It's early September, so it still *feels* like summer, but there's a hue in the air that tells me fall is fast approaching. I watch an elderly couple strolling down the sidewalk as Kinsley chats with the rental owner. This isn't a disaster—but it is a logistical irritation.

Especially because the first order of business I had planned was getting Kinsley naked and pressed up against the wall of the first shower I saw.

"Mm-hmm," Kinsley is saying on the phone. "Right. That makes sense."

Kinsley's frown grows deeper the longer she's on the phone. When she hangs up, she heaves a big sigh.

"A sewer line ruptured, and they have to fix it before they can let us in. They estimate it will be done by Thursday."

"Thursday."

"Yeah." She looks as unhappy as I feel. We watch each other for a few moments while the logistics begin to unfold in the air between us. It's Sunday. We won't be able to get into the rental until the day before our rehearsal.

"But that's fine, right?" I'm trying to be optimistic here.

"Yeah. It just means we have to...you know..." Her periwinkle gaze meets mine, followed by a hard swallow. "Figure out where we'll stay."

Right. The entire drama we were hoping to avoid.

A tense half hour passes as we discuss options. If this were any other trip during any other week, it wouldn't matter. But the other fancy rental options in the area are all booked—some, I'm sure, by incoming members of our family. And as Kinsley soon reveals, other plans hinge on the original plan of this rental. As in, the cocktail party that Hazel has planned for our families is slated to occur at the lakefront rental, which is why Kinsley gracelessly bats down my idea to just get a little hotel room and be done with it.

"Let's just stay where it's easiest," I finally say.

"My parents," she says, and then winces. "But they said some of the family will be arriving as of Wednesday. They might not have space."

"We can go to my mom and dad's."

Kinsley nibbles on her bottom lip, nodding at me. "Okay. Let's just do that."

"Great." I kick the van into reverse, backing out of our lakefront parking spot. If it was so great, why did I have a knot in my stomach? "That'll work out perfectly."

"Just make sure we get the room we always get," Kinsley says with a meaningful look. I know what she's getting at—the bedroom where it all began, connected bathroom with stand-up shower and all.

"Of course. Like I'd let my fiancée suffer with a sub-standard room assignment," I scoff, holding her hand as I navigate us toward my parents' house. When we reach the tree-lined subdivision boasting tightly packed homes in various stages of summer repose—some with kayaks propped against the garage door, others with fishing boats stowed in parked trailers—a whoosh of contentment flows through me. *I'm home.*

There's nothing more comforting than coming back to the streets where I grew up. We both love Bayshore for so many reasons, but for me, there's no topping this: the relaxed, lake vibe that can put you in summer mode, no matter how stressed life gets, no matter what's on the to-do list. And specifically for us, right now, it's helping me forget the maroon monstrosity I'm driving. The fact that our house rental might be currently filling with sewage. The endless array of possible failures our business might be headed for while we're unavailable.

I can forget it all while I'm in lake mode.

Mom is halfway out the door by the time I pull into the driveway. I swear she's got a radar that alerts her whenever one of her sons is within fifty feet of the front door. Kinsley is out of the van first, and Mom sends her a small smile, squeezing the sides of Kinsley's arms before sweeping toward me. It's a stark improvement over that first frosty greeting three years ago, when Mom could barely hide her distaste for Kinsley during that trip for Grammy Ethel's funeral. And though Kinsley has a point that our families might have been secretly hopeful we'd end things in the ensuing years, I'd like to think my mom has come to accept—maybe even like—our pairing.

"There's my boy," Mom says as she smashes my cheeks between her hands and inspects my face. Her dark brown hair is pulled into a low bun, and she looks like she's been baking, based on the flour across the front of her shirt. Then she pulls me into a tight hug, letting out a long sigh.

"How was the trip?" she asked, ushering us both toward the house. "How is the rental house? Are you hungry?"

I lace my fingers through Kinsley's as we follow her down the stone path leading to the front door. "I could go for a snack," I admit.

"Always down for snacks," Kinsley echoes.

"But actually, we had a little snafu with the rental." Inside, the wooden floorboards and lakeside accoutrements further restore my calm. How can things go wrong when wrapped up in the warm embrace of your childhood home? "There was a sewer issue, so we can't get in there until Thursday."

"Oh no." Mom tuts, rummaging in the fridge as Kinsley and I sit on the stools at the kitchen island. "So what's the plan? Do you need to stay here?"

"That's what we were hoping," I say, reaching for Kinsley's hand.

"Of course, honey. You know you can stay here whenever you want. As long as you want." My mom sends us a reassuring smile as she brings over a few blocks of cheese. She grabs a box of crackers before she dives into cutting out bite-size chunks of Monterey jack, aged cheddar, and Port Salut. "No questions asked."

Kinsley smiles as she reaches for a cheese and cracker combo. "We really appreciate that. I was worried you might have promised the extra rooms to family members coming in from out of town or something."

"Is that what happened?" Mom's brows lift, as though the realization is creeping into her. "Honey, our children come first. I would kick Uncle Pat out of the spare room if my Connor needed it. Especially for his wedding week."

"Well, I didn't mean to say that—"

"We didn't even—" I begin at the same time.

"It's okay. No questions asked." My mom looks oddly satisfied, and I realize we've inadvertently played into the Cabana-Daly rift, even though we were prepared and aware and actively avoiding this. My mom has used this detail as quiet confirmation of the Daly family superiority. We've taken one step back.

I steer the conversation to other topics—the state of wedding plans, how the business has been doing, what our honeymoon reservations entail—and by the time we've finished the cheese and cracker platter, my mom urges us to go pick a room upstairs and settle in.

We do as we're told, carting our luggage upstairs to our middle room paradise with the connected bathroom. Kinsley flops back on the bed with a contented sigh. "Home sweet home, for now."

"First home of about six," I say with a snort as I compulsively check my email. *Just in case* something needs my attention.

"Put that phone down, mister," she warns me. "I can tell you're checking work email."

I smirk at her as I pocket it. "How can you tell?"

"You get this very specific look on your face, like you're waiting to get punched."

"Fine. You're right. It's a hard habit to break, though."

Kinsley starts to respond but gets interrupted by her own phone ringing. She picks it up swiftly, setting it to speaker phone so she can continue splaying out as she speaks. "Hello, Mother."

"Hi, honey. Are you in yet? How's the house?"

"Oh, we had a change of plans already," she says. I busy myself with opening my suitcase while she talks, though I'm listening to every word. "The house had an emergency so we can't get in there until Thursday, so we're at Connor's parents' house until then."

An odd silence fills the room.

"Mom? Are you there?" Kinsley asks.

"Yes, I'm here." There's some rustling on the other end of the phone. "Why didn't you come here? We'd have loved to have you."

"I know, I just figured that since Aunt Bethany is planning to visit as of Wednesday, that—"

"But we have other rooms," her mom interjects.

"Yes, but Kestrel said she's planning on coming home early, too," Kinsley says. "You guys are gonna have a full house, and we don't want to get in the way."

"You'd never be in the way," her mom says. "And I don't know where you got that idea."

"Mom," Kinsley begins with a sigh.

"You're the bride," Lisa goes on. "You should be at your mother's house."

Kinsley runs her tongue over her top teeth, staring at the ceiling. "I don't see why it matters. I wasn't going to be staying with you anyway."

"But you'd rather stay over *there*?"

Kinsley covers her eyes with a hand. "No, Mom. It's not that. Listen, we made the decision on the fly. It just seemed easiest. Can we leave it at that?"

Lisa lets out a terse sigh. "Fine. When will you be stopping by?"

The two chat a little bit more about logistics that don't involve sleeping arrangements, and by the time they hang up, Kinsley pushes onto her elbows to pin me with an unamused look.

"Is it too soon to start drinking?"

"Babe, it's way past five o'clock in Bayshore, which means no. We're right on time."

She claps her hands together. "Good. Let's go to Hi-5's for a pre-dealing-with-any-parents-again drink."

And she's right. We're thirty minutes into Bayshore and our parents are already proving they don't plan on making this easy.

Which means that we need to get extra crafty in the coming week.

# CHAPTER THREE

KINSLEY

It's Tuesday, which marks the very first day of our bona fide wedding week celebration. I should be bubbling over with excitement and good-natured party vibes, but I'm not.

Because really, I'm dreading the moment that the Cabana and Daly heads of household finally convene under one roof.

Connor and I did a good job of divvying up our first day in Bayshore between both families and plenty of recreational lake-gazing. We even took the boat out once for a sunset trip and performed a mock ceremony for only us with the perch as our witnesses. I would have been happy to leave that as the formal wedding ceremony, but I don't think it'll hold up in court...though really, I don't know unless I try.

We're the first to the party, because we're technically Annette and Damon's housemates now. I glide down the staircase in a maroon wraparound dress paired with matching wedge heels and some funky earrings I picked up at a thrift store in San Diego. They're lightning bolts, which I'm hoping will turn into my secret super-power should the need arise.

Connor is in the hallway when I come downstairs, and his eyes light up when he sees me. "Aww, you match the van," he tells me, pulling me into a hug.

"Wh—th—" That comment hardly qualifies as a sweet nothing. "Thank you?"

His grin is ear-to-ear as he looks me over. "We should go back upstairs."

"Family-sized vehicles really turn you on, huh?"

"I'm ready to need a family-sized vehicle with the way your ass looks in this dress," he says, turning me to the side to get a better look.

I swat his arm. "Guests are going to be arriving soon, so our passenger van roleplay will have to wait until later." Still, I push up onto my toes and give him a big kiss on the lips. Because how could I not kiss this man at every possible chance? "I love you."

"Love you too, Sunny-kins," he says, reaching down to squeeze an ass cheek. He follows me into the kitchen, where I left things in a state of half-preparation earlier. A knock on the front door sounds, which Connor goes to answer while I get back to party preparations. A moment later, I hear the sonorous tones of Hazel's voice as she greets Connor, followed by Grayson's spirited tenor. A moment later, we're all hugging and greeting each other in the kitchen, and Hazel leaps into action.

"I can't tell you how excited I've been for this cocktail party," she confesses as she slides next to me, immediately getting busy with arranging a half-finished charcuterie board.

"I'm pumped to try these new recipes Grayson claims to be a pro at," I tell her, dumping olives into a serving bowl for our guest bartender to use.

"Don't get your hopes *too* high on that one," Hazel says in a hushed voice. Her ruby red lips are curved into a mischievous smile. "He's been practicing, I'll give him that much."

"Hey, as long as it contains alcohol, right?"

She peers around the kitchen. "Where are Annette and Damon?"

"I think upstairs getting ready still," I say, my stomach twisting into the familiar sailor's knot. And then, my biggest worry rolls off my tongue: "I didn't tell my parents the party would be at Connor's parents' house. I just sent them the address without telling them what it was."

"That shouldn't be a problem, though, right? They already planned on coming when it was going to be at the rental."

"Right." Still, though, it feels like a problem. But maybe it's just me being paranoid. Anxious. Unnecessarily negative.

"But you're worried," Hazel finishes for me.

"Yeah." I muster a weak laugh. "I know I signed on to this, and I'm committed to seeing it through. I just wonder—"

"Oh, Gray!" Annette's voice lights up the kitchen, and Hazel snaps on a bright smile. Our conversation is officially dead in the water. I'm not going to utter another word while Annette is in the same room, much less when I'm trying to usher in relaxed cocktail party vibes.

"Hazel! You look beautiful," Annette coos as she gives Hazel a side hug. Almost as an afterthought, she adds, "And I love that dress Kinsley."

*See, Kins? She's trying.* There's my voice of reason. The voice eager to reassure me that having arch-nemeses on the same private property after thirty years of hostile avoidance will absolutely end in a positive manner. *If she's trying with you, she'll try with your parents.*

But honestly, it's not Annette I'm worried about.

It's good ol' Mom & Dad Cabana that have me tense and arranging pepperonis on the charcuterie board as if a panel of judges will be involved.

"Thanks, Annette," I say brightly, trying to remind her how much she's come to not-hate me over the past three years, as if my smile alone might be enough to anchor me in the upcoming stormy sea that is sure to unmoor her from whatever rosy feelings she might hold for me.

Annette joins the ranks as we get things ready. London and Dom show up, and after a round of hugs, we collectively take a ten-minute break to coo at London's enormous belly. They just got back from their own honeymoon; their wedding was only last month.

"When are you due?" I ask London, rubbing my palm over the big curve of her belly after she told me I could touch.

"Three more weeks," she says with a sigh. She's as sparklingly beautiful as ever, but I can see the exhaustion in her eyes. "I don't know how I'm going to make it. I swear this baby weighs twenty pounds already."

"Five pounds eight ounces," Dominic corrects quietly at her side. "As of the last OB visit, at least."

"Didn't they teach you in medical school not to correct a pregnant lady?" she asks with a wry grin for her husband, and then pushes onto her toes to press a kiss to his cheek.

The rest of the guest list includes Daly family friends, my own parents, and a smattering of old high school friends who are still in the area. Time ticks on. More and more friendly faces enter the house, and Annette and Damon are tucked into the backyard holding cocktails while they chat with guests. And then, the entire guest list has arrived—minus Maverick for work reasons, and Weston and Nova for international reasons...and my parents. I keep watching the front door and checking my phone. *When will Mom and Dad get here?*

I've finished an entire martini by the time my phone buzzes with an incoming call. *Mom.* I nearly choke on the olive I was biting into and hurry to answer it.

"Yes? Hello?"

"Kinsley."

"Mom. What's up? Where are you?"

There's an unnerving silence, but I can't tell if it's because I'm caught in the middle of a conversation between Grayson and Connor about renovation projects, or if there really is an iciness coming through the line.

"Mom?"

"We're outside," Mom says, but she doesn't sound happy. "Can you come out here please?"

"Sure. Of course." I swipe my phone off and tell Connor where I'm going, then I hurry out the front door. The world outside is starkly different from the happy, buzzing bubble in the Daly house. Out here, I remember there's an entire world of people not celebrating my upcoming marriage.

And maybe my parents don't plan to join the bubble.

Mom and Dad are standing on the sidewalk—not technically Daly property. Mom's got her arms crossed, and Dad's got his hands stuffed in his pockets, jingling keys.

"What's wrong? You can come in, you know..." I begin, trying to act as though there's not been a dark cloud between these families for thirty years.

"You did *not* tell us this mixer was going to be at Annette's house," my mom hisses, as if she's trying to stay quiet lest the clapboard siding of the Daly house itself can hear her.

"We had to switch it here because of the issues with the rental," I explain, looking between my parents. They look as grim and stern as if I'd just told them we'd be parachuting to the cocktail party after choosing one finger to cut off with a knife. "I told you, the sewer was backed up or something, and we can't get in until Thursday."

"We know," my dad explains, sounding like he's far past exasperated. "But a little forewarning would have been nice."

"We knew we'd be *seeing them* here; we didn't know we'd be frolicking in their backyard," Mom adds.

I'm taken aback. "I don't think frolicking is on the agenda—"

"Hey, guys!" Hazel's voice cuts through the tense sidewalk discussion. I turn, more grateful than ever to see the brunette bombshell. She glides over to us, practically floating despite the stilettos, a bright smile on her ruby red lips. "You ready to party?"

My mom offers a genuine smile to Hazel, and my dad gives a gruff "Hello." They're technically each other's competition—the two biggest names in realty in Bayshore are *Hazel* and *Cabana*—but they each have their faithful clientele and have even helped each other out in the past.

"We're a little surprised by the venue choice," my mom says in a way that betrays approximately zero of the tension from ten seconds ago. "But yes, we're ready."

There we go. They just needed to get it out of their system.

"It's a gorgeous party so far," Hazel enthuses. I could kiss her for being the mediator here. Maybe she knew, and that's why she came out. "My husband Grayson is mixing the drinks, and he's getting pretty creative, so you won't be disappointed."

My dad grunts as the four of us begin a slow trek toward the front door. Still, I can feel their hesitation as the front door of the Daly house looms closer. Hazel sweeps inside after sending one last encouraging smile our way, and I pause at the screen door with my hand on knob.

"You guys can do this for me, right?"

Mom still looks strained, but she nods. I take a deep breath and open the door, leading the way. Note to self: pretending the resentful stalemate between our families does not exist is not the best way to handle party planning. But it's too late now. Because *Here we are, Dalys...* and there's still five more days of this pre-planned torture ahead of us.

"Oooh, look who it is!" Connor is extra chipper when my parents walk into the kitchen behind me. He's never been *this* happy to see them, but I can tell he's staving off tension as much as I am. Hazel calls them over to the makeshift bartending stand Gray created at the kitchen island. He's even got a dishtowel slung over one shoulder.

"What'll it be, Cabanas?" Gray asks good-naturedly. I stand off to my parents' side, wringing my hands, while Connor heads them up on the other side. We're practically boxing them in. Making sure they stay and *enjoy themselves, goddammit.*

"Just water for me," my mom says, and Dad asks for a light beer. Connor and I share a nervous smile behind their backs.

"So how's work been going recently?" Hazel swoops in from across the countertop to chat with my dad. If there's one thing he loves to talk about, it's real estate, so I'm relieved when he and Hazel fall into the black hole of investment property discussions.

Which means my Mom needs to be distracted. I spot London across the kitchen, gesturing at her to come over. She waddles our way, brushing blonde hair out of her face. "Mom, have you met London before? She recently married Connor's oldest brother Dom. She's due in three weeks."

"Two, if I'm lucky," London says, extending her hand to my mom. "Nice to meet you."

"My mom used to work at Bayshore General Hospital in Labor and Delivery," I offer, trying to find some spark of a conversation that will encourage my parents to have a good time. And if there's anything I know my mom can't say no to, it's new moms. "My mom's delivered her fair share of babies, that's for sure."

"Oh, too bad you won't be there," London said, rubbing her palms underneath her belly. "I'd love to have all the experience I can get on my side."

"You'll do fine, I can already tell," my mom says with a wink. "Let me guess. You're having a girl."

London shrieks with surprise, marking the official beginning of pleasant conversation. *Score.* Some of the binds around my heart loosen, and I slink toward Connor, secretly giving him a high five.

"Parental integration underway," I say out of the side of my mouth as we stand at the perimeter, admiring the group handiwork. I'm thanking Hazel and London in my head while Connor goes to get another round of mixed drinks from Grayson. We manage to slip into conversation with some of the family friends nearby. One round of drinks turns into two. My dad begins talking to Grayson after a while, presumably about investment property plans, based on the way I keep overhearing the phrase 'incredible potential.' Connor is holding his third empty martini glass, slinking past my mom to go drop it off in the kitchen when suddenly there's the undeniable sound of glass shattering.

My mom reels back, gasping, staring at the floor. "I'm so sorry!"

Connor looks stunned, looking between his hand and the remains of his glass on the floor. The party goes quiet suddenly, just as Annette Daly mutters from across the room, "I bet she did it on purpose."

Voices swell a bit, filling the lapse of noise, but my heart is racing. My mom stiffens. Connor's got the deer-in-headlights look. And then suddenly, that impassive mask is back on my mom's face. The one she always used during my childhood when the topic of the Dalys came up. Like she was using every ounce of her internal strength not to say something awful or maybe even slap a bitch.

"Honey." My mom grabs my dad's wrist after he and Grayson sink back into conversation. "I forgot about that appointment we have."

His brows furrow. "What appointment?"

"For the boat."

My dad blinks, and then he nods. "That's right. I can't believe the time." He clears his throat, discarding his beer can.

"Honey, it's time for us to leave," Mom says to me, not looking at all sad about it. She pulls me into a hug before I can protest. "We need to start getting the boat ready for storage."

"Oh. Okay." I hug each of them in turn, a little heartbroken. What the hell had happened from across the room? It was like our mothers had waged, fought, and resolved an entire private, silent battle, and my mom was the one forced to slink away. I wave as my parents take their leave, noticing the death glare that our mothers exchange just before my mom slips out of the house.

"Connor," I hiss, cornering him in the kitchen. "That was some Drama with a capital D, and I don't like it one bit."

"Babe. I know. I was the one who dropped the glass, too."

"This was supposed to be fun. But our parents are *ruining it*."

Connor crumples slightly, taking my face in his hands. "They aren't ruining it. They can't. We won't let them."

"Were we so wrong to think they'd be able to act like adults and move on from the past?"

Connor purses his lips before he answers, and an unbearably long time goes by. So much time, in fact, that we burst out laughing.

"Yes, we were wrong," he finally answers. "But you know what? This is the week they have to make an effort on our behalf." He leans in to press a soft kiss to my lips. "Let's give 'em hell."

# CHAPTER FOUR

CONNOR

My alarm goes off at an ungodly hour the next morning. I grapple for my phone in the dim light, struggling to remember why I set it and what happened to make my mouth so dry. Then the realization crests in waves: I am hungover from yesterday's cocktail party, and the next item on my to-do list is a men's fishing trip.

"Nnnggghrrrgh." Kinsley swats at me, eyes pinched shut. "Turn it."

"I am." My voice is gritty as I fumble to turn the alarm off. It's seven thirty. Why did we schedule a fishing trip this early the day after the cocktail party? Only the wedding planning gods know, I suppose. I roll out of bed just as my phone buzzes with an incoming text.

*GRAYSON: Hey, I'm good to come on the fishing trip right?*

I stumble into the attached bathroom and flip the light switch, squinting against the influx of light. At this point, I can't imagine why anyone wants to go on a fishing trip.

*CONNOR: Of cours. E.*
*GRAYSON: You still drunk?*
*CONNOR: Yesg*

I grip the side of the sink as I brush my teeth, staring at myself, trying to rally. I don't feel puke-sick, just more like soul-sucked-out-of-my-body-with-a-straw sick. I splash lots of water on my face, lick my lips, and then guzzle water straight from the tap.

I manage to dress myself and stumble downstairs. My dad and Grayson are already there. Gray immediately hands me a mug of coffee.

"Drink up, brother. You're gonna need it."

"These fish are ready to bite," my dad says. Fishing is one of the few activities he loves, beyond making money and remaining in his job as CEO of Bayshore General Hospital. "And if we're lucky, we'll find lunch."

"Oh, sure," Grayson teases, "like you'll be first in line to make a perch sandwich from scratch?"

"Never said we'd find lunch and make it ourselves," Dad shoots back, a shit-eating grin on his face. "Somebody else can goddamn well make it for us."

I snort before I chug the entire contents of the coffee mug. I hand it back to Grayson and jerk my chin to signify 'more.' As he fills it up for me, because my multitasking functions are limited to breathing and standing, I check my phone.

*DOM: I'm heading straight to the boat dock.*

*CONNOR: Let me know if Jack shows up. We'll be on our way soon.*

I let out a rumbling sigh after the effort of sending that text. Then I decide I need more water. I head for the cupboard and serve myself an overflowing glass.

"Connor's in rough shape," Grayson says.

I grunt. "Why do you sound happy about it, *bartender*?"

Gray smirks. "Listen, I might have overpoured a few drinks. But we had a damn good time."

That we did. Including a late-night pizza delivery and a surprise round of Cards Against Humanity with Hazel, Grayson, Mom, and a few of the high school friends who stuck around. I've never seen my mom so overjoyed to win a round, especially when the phrase that got her points was: *What are my parents hiding from me? Lance Armstrong's missing testicle.*

"The fresh air will put you right," Dad says, delivering a near-fatal clap on my back. I stumble forward—the man is a giant—and a headache begins to sprout.

"Let me grab an aspirin before we go," I mutter, rummaging in the cabinets before I find the blessed medicine.

Once we're all loaded into the car, the drive to the boat launch isn't long. At this stupidly early hour on a Wednesday morning, Bayshore is beautiful and brimming with energy. People are strolling along the boardwalk, enjoying the crisp September morning air without a hangover. As we roll into the huge parking lot of the boat launch, some clarity returns to me. Maybe that's thanks to the caffeine and gallon of water I consumed. But when I spot Dom—and Jack Cabana—lingering near the docks, I remember again what I signed up for. A fishing trip with the men. Including two men who actively dislike each other.

"We're gonna have a good time," I declare, as though this will help ensure the outcome. My dad grunts as he heads to the back of his SUV and begins hauling out the fishing equipment.

"I'm gonna catch some fish," he replies.

"It'll be nice to get on the water one last time," Gray adds, rummaging through equipment. I grab extra for Dom, and then we're all headed toward Dom and Jack. Jack tips his fishing cap to us as we approach, which I'll assume is the most greeting my father will get from the man. Dom squeezes my shoulder, looking intently at my face.

"You need more water."

"Thanks, Dr. Dom," I mutter, passing off the fishing equipment. "But I drank plenty of water before I came."

Jack Cabana heads down the dock where his fishing boat is tied off. I know he has another larger boat, but it's a ski boat, and therefore must not be used for fishing, apparently. As five adult men, we'll fit, but it might be tight. No big deal. After all, this is a bonding activity. And there's nothing that bonds men more than cramped quarters and waiting for fish.

"Little small," my dad says as we stop in front.

Jack turns slightly. "We can use your boat, if you'd like."

My dad doesn't have a boat, so this qualifies as a level seven burn.

We climb aboard silently. I'm watching Grayson, who is watching me with a look that says *Yeah, I heard that too, and this could still get ugly, but maybe it won't.* At least, that's what I'm hoping the look is telling me. Because if he's urging me to jump ship now and cancel the fishing trip, it's too late. We've piled inside, fishing equipment clattering onto the long benches, and before we know it, Jack has untied us and we've pushed off. The motor rumbles to life a moment later, and my dad, who is sitting at the bow, grimaces visibly, as though the Cabana engine has also offended him somehow.

"This is going well," I murmur to Dom as we move slowly through the no-wake zone, out into the barely-choppy waters of Briggs Bay. I don't know if it's a manic proclamation or a thinly-veiled question.

Dom doesn't respond—merely frowns in response.

Once we're out of the no-wake zone from the boat launch, Jack guns it and the boat kicks into high gear. Crisp, morning air rushes past me, putting a smile on my face. The air is curing my hangover; if

I imagine hard enough, I can see it dissolving behind me in the wind as the lake air sucks it out of me.

Except once we start hitting the waves in a rhyth-mic *thup-thup-thup*, my stomach doesn't abide by the hang-over-sucked-out-of-me narrative. It begins to churn. *Badly*. I grimace out at the beautiful lake. *This is fine. Everything is fine.*

I'm counting down the minutes until Jack shows a sign of slowing down the boat. Meanwhile, my butt cheeks are clenched and I'm counseling myself on how sick I don't feel. One hundred percent not sick. Absolutely not at the precipice of vomiting.

Finally, blessedly, we're coming up on a little bridge near the eastern edge of Bayshore, which is a popular spot for fishermen to gather. We're definitely not the first to the party; other fishing boats already float along the perimeter of the bridge. Jack throttles down, hard, and I'm pitched forward. I almost puke in my mouth. Goddamn Grayson and his experimental cocktails.

Jack maneuvers us into a prime fishing spot. Far enough away from other boats, but still close to the popular rocky area the fish love to congregate in. We begin readying our reels. Grayson glances at me while he grabs for some bait.

"You don't look so hot, bro."

"I fully blame you."

He smirks. "I think you're just getting old, my man. Can't handle your liquor anymore."

"I'm the youngest one here; why aren't you two feeling the same?"

"I was too busy getting you fools drunk," Gray says.

"And I actually know my limits," Dom piped up.

"Thanks again, Dr. Dom, for your input." Older brothers never stopped being annoying know-it-alls.

As we talk, the fathers remain conspicuously silent on opposite ends of the fishing boat.

"How's Kinsley feeling today?" Gray asks.

"Lucky," I tell him, "since she gets to sleep it off."

My dad sucks on his teeth as the line jerks. A moment later, he reels in a fish. "First one."

Jack looks over his shoulder, then down at his fishless, water-filled bucket. I think I hear a gunshot somewhere in the recesses of my mind. My brothers and I continue casual conversation while the two men at the opposite ends of the boat begin the most intense battle of silent fishing ever waged. Jack flops a wriggling fish into his bucket. Then Dad pops another one into his. Jack calls out the new number each time he adds a fish. Meanwhile, my brothers and I are collectively at "one half," if you count the fish that Dominic had and then lost.

"We are sucking," Grayson hisses, yet makes no move to improve. Admittedly, this is one competition I don't want to get involved in. Even Dom, biologically the most competitive man in the world after our father, is opting out of this battle.

"Ten," Jack calls out nonchalantly, followed by a wet flop in his bucket.

My dad huffs and pushes to his feet. He stalks the length of the boat, headed for the extra reel he brought, just as Jack swivels and launches toward his own box. The two men collide in the way that can only happen when you are actively trying to avoid looking at someone. It's almost comical. Except my brothers and I are wincing through it.

"Watch where you're going," Jack says gruffly.

"Same to you," Dad shoots back. "Didn't realize going for my reel was a crime on this boat."

"Not sure it's gonna help much," Jack says with a smirk. "It's a good thing your family isn't counting on you feeding them with your haul today."

My organs begin to squish together in discomfort, which just makes me more nauseous overall. I am desperate to derail this slowly escalating brawl.

"I don't think we'd even want to eat such tiny—" I start, trying to sound as lighthearted and neutral as I can muster around the edges of my hangover.

"Guess there isn't such a thing as fishing for fun, huh?" Dad growls.

"Not when you're barking out the count like a carny over there," Jack shoots back.

Dad steps closer to Jack, who has since balled his fists. Something about the escalating tension turns the knot of nausea in my gut into a brick, and everything feels all-around icky.

"Thought that was how you liked things to run on your dinghy," Dad spits. "Say it so everyone can hear it. Not like I need to talk real loud in the five square feet on board here. Thought you specialized in real estate. Must not be in the watercraft kind."

Jack laughs bitterly, shaking his head as he loads up another shiner to his reel. "Still such a class act, I see, Damon. Even after all these years. You know, I should have known better than to offer up my boat to anyone with the Daly name. Hell, you might come back with that bucket of fish a week later and claim it isn't yours after all."

My brothers and I exchange deer-in-headlights looks while Dad's face goes tight, a crazy glint in his eye.

"What did you say to me?"

"You know exactly what I said to you," Jack shoots back. "If that wife of yours decides she doesn't want it, she'll probably come back and say it was mine to begin with."

Something snaps in the air, maybe the final strand of goodwill that we'd all foolishly thought existed. "How *dare* you speak about my wife like that," Dad barks.

Things happen quickly then. Dad advances toward Jack with that insane look in his eyes, which causes Gray to bolt to his feet and insert himself between the fathers. Dom jolts to standing at exactly the same time Jack pushes Gray out of the way in a bid to get at my dad.

Gray stumbles to the side, trips over the bench, and flies off the edge of the boat. Dom's sudden movement makes the boat sway crazily, which gives my own stomach the final push it needs to eject its contents. I projectile puke off the other side of the boat just as Gray's giant *splash* echoes through the morning air.

"Oh my Godddd," I groan, hanging my head over the side of the boat as another round of experimental cocktails churn upward from the depths of my gut.

There's shouting, then, and a lot of splashing. My eyes are watering, and I'm just trying to get all of this scourge out of me before I go to help my brother. Besides, Dom's got it. He's shouting Gray's name while my Dad keeps repeating "Grab this ledge. Grab this ledge."

Even Jack is doing his part, tossing a rope out to Gray in the event that he goes under.

"Guys, I know how to fucking swim," Gray says as he paddles to the back of the boat.

He hauls himself onto the back of the fishing boat and sits there, letting himself drip for a few moments.

"Grayson, I'm sorry," Jack says. "That was uncalled for. I shouldn't have pushed you."

It's an apology for pushing—not for the other cryptic thing he said, which conjured some Ouija-board-style demons out of my dad.

"Hey, it's fine," he says, running a hand through his Lake Erie-drenched tresses. "But I'm pretty sure we fucked up the fishing for the rest of the day. Might as well call it, boys."

I splash some lake water on my face before I haul myself back onto the bench. Everyone is quiet and tense as Grayson wrings out his clothes. Some of the other fisherman are looking our way, shaking their heads. But my unexpected puke therapy has bestowed some clarity upon me. I look between the two men, squinting.

"When are you two going to get over this shit?"

A stunned silence ripples across the boat, but it only prompts me to continue.

"I don't even know what happened or why it still matters, but now seems like as good a time as ever to just sit down and hash it out," I say. Wow, that projectile cocktail really *did* cleanse me. "This might be the only chance to save this wedding that my fiancée is slowly becoming less and less excited about because of this bullshit."

Jack crumples at that.

"Son—" my dad begins.

"She should be excited," Jack says at the same time. "And it's going to be a great wedding." He starts the engine again. My brothers make quick work of putting away the lines and reels. "We just know better than to try to fix something that can't be fixed."

"Because you two have ever tried?" I ask, looking at my dad.

He looks wearier than I've ever seen him. "It's not worth trying."

"That's the spirit," I mutter, grabbing for my reel.

We've accomplished something today, though it's the opposite of what I intended.

Instead of bringing our fathers together, I've revealed that the rift between them is deeper than anyone imagined.

# CHAPTER FIVE

KINSLEY

It's Thursday, *finally*. It means a lot of things—like moving into our cute lakefront rental house which thankfully does *not* smell like plumbing issues. Also, there's only one day until the rehearsal. And maybe most importantly: it's my final dress fitting.

My friend Lena has flown in from San Diego. She quit E-bid not long after I was fired, which meant that we quickly roped her into the fold at Wizard Initiatives. Our friendship has been going strong and steady ever since. On today's docket is a girl's day: Lena, Hazel, my mother, and I, convening upon the luxurious Necessary Needles bridal shop in downtown Bayshore for the final fitting and some complementary beverages.

I want today to be as relaxed as possible, especially since I'm still reeling from what Connor told me happened yesterday morning on the lake. I haven't talked to my parents about it. And honestly, I'm not sure if I should just pretend that my fiancé didn't puke off the side of my dad's fishing boat. Is that what pre-wedding etiquette dictates? There is no handbook for this sort of thing, at least not one that Emily Post has publicly shared (and yes, I checked).

"Oooh, it feels so nice in here," Hazel says as we breeze into the cool interior of Necessary Needles. It's excessively hot today, so the cool air and luxury before us is very welcome. It's part showroom for a limited collection of wedding dresses, part appointment-only alterations and fittings. Two long sofas line the mirrored area I am led to by the Necessary Needler herself, Nancy. Lena relaxes into one of the cream-colored couches, her jet-black bob contrasting with the couch. My mom and Hazel sink into the other. Everyone sighs with relief as Nancy returns to the fitting area with a tray of champagne flutes and a cheese platter.

"This is the life," Lena says, kicking up her feet.

"I like to make dress fittings *fun*," Nancy oozes as she passes around the champagne. I am already standing on the fitting podium, a full two feet above the ground and on display, even though I'm still dressed in my street clothes.

"This is exactly the sort of fun I like to have," I tell her, taking a grateful sip. It took me all of yesterday to recover from our cocktail party; I'm lucky I hadn't been invited on the men's fishing trip, because otherwise there would have been two of us doubled over the edge, which I know Emily Post absolutely would not have suggestions for in her books.

Once drinks are served and my audience is happily munching on cheese cubes, Nancy calls me away from the podium and into the dressing room, where my wedding dress is waiting.

And yes, I get a little emotional when I see it again. It's been a while. And well, the champagne hit me fast. I skipped breakfast and almost skipped lunch during my hectic day thus far. So I'm surprised and maybe a little embarrassed when a tear slips out.

"Wow. Hi. There she is." I finger the lace edge of my bodice. "I forgot how pretty she was."

"It's a gorgeous dress," Nancy reassures me. "And I can't wait to see how the alterations work. Just let me know when you need me to zip you up." She leaves me to my own devices, and I smile at my watery reflection in the mirror while I shed my clothes and step into the dress. I pause there, a hand on my chest, looking myself up and down. Is this really happening? I'm getting married in *two days*. To *Connor Daly*. The man who stole my heart, changed my life, and puked off my dad's boat during a skirmish.

I've never loved that man more than in this exact moment.

I blink away more tears, fanning my face before calling to Nancy to zip me. She looks supremely pleased when she pulls the curtain aside, beaming at me in the way only a proud mother or accomplished seamstress can. I follow her out of the dressing room like this is the wedding itself. When I round the corner, the three women gasp in unison.

"Kinsley!" Lena screeches. "You look *amazing!*"

"That dress," Hazel says, a hand to her chest, "is gorgeous."

"Oh, honey." My mom's chin is trembling, and she sweeps to her feet. At least I'm not the only one crying now. She pulls me into a hug, and I'm yet again at a loss for what to do in this situation. *Emily Post, where the fuck are you?* I feel like sobbing in my mother's arms during the dress fitting is not entirely appropriate, but who knows—maybe Nancy sees this daily.

"I love it," I say, looking down at myself once my mom has slipped back into her seat. I reach for my champagne and down the rest in one gulp. "I could not love a dress more, in fact."

Lena and Hazel coo over the details—the plunging back, the satin train, the lace-up corset style bodice complete with feathers, lace, and beads. Nancy guides me back to the podium and positions me just so, staring at my reflection in the angled mirrors in front of of us. Then she notices the state of our champagne flutes.

"Are we ready for seconds?" she asks.

"Yes!" Lena says triumphantly, her glass in the air.

While Nancy whisks away our empties, I twirl back and forth on the podium, admiring my reflection. "Mom, take some pictures on my phone, will you?"

"Of course, honey." She rummages through my purse, producing my phone a moment later. She tuts lovingly as she takes photos from all possible angles. When Nancy returns with more champagne, everyone cheers. I hold my newly refilled flute in one hand while Nancy gets to work on the last-minute adjustments.

"Saturday is going to be so amazing, I can feel it already," Hazel says.

"You think so?" I ask, meaning it to be lighthearted. But too late I realize the fear beneath my own question. It's more than just pre-wedding jitters. It's entire family calamities.

"Of course," Hazel says. "With you two getting married, and this dress involved, it can only be a fairytale."

"Says the woman who actually had the fairytale wedding," I tease her. To Lena, I say, "You should have seen her wedding this past spring. It was at the Bayshore Theatre and totally gorgeous. She had a mauve wedding dress, even."

"It fit the theme better," Hazel says.

Lena and Hazel talk a little bit about the particulars of the wedding—Lena tends toward all things dark and macabre, so Hazel's wedding gives her hope she can pull off something similar someday—while I watch Nancy gather fabric and take measurements. My mom sinks into her phone, leaving me thinking back on what I meant by my comment.

*I'm not looking forward to Saturday.*

The thought ripples through me like an oil slick. Unpleasant, thick, hard to get rid of. But it's true: I'm not looking forward to my own wedding. I'm a nervous wreck, in fact, and the closer we get to the big day, the more our families prove that they cannot be trusted around one another.

If my dad could push Grayson off a fishing boat on Wednesday, what will our families be capable of come Saturday?

I try to stuff the anxieties back into the Pandora's box they sprang from, but it's not easy. Not when I'm in this dress, surrounded by all the trappings of a wedding, watching Nancy fuss over my bodice. I down the rest of my champagne. The alcohol buzzes through my veins.

Hazel and Lena start talking about Grayson after a little bit, and it's at that point my buzz has transformed into drunkenness, kind of like the way Peter Parker turns into Spiderman.

"Hazel," I blurt. "Be honest with me. Grayson's not upset about what happened yesterday, is he?"

Hazel's eyes go wide, and I realize I've broken a self-imposed rule: *Do not talk about the awkward family shit in mixed company.* But, well, too late.

"He's fine," Hazel reassures me.

"No hard feelings? For real?"

"Girl, I promise you." Hazel bats away the suggestion. "He told me when he got home that he'd been wanting one last dip in the lake anyway."

Lena snorts. "Oh my God. What happened?"

Tension stretches across the fitting room. My mom dips her head, and I can tell it's up to me to answer this one. "My dad pushed him into the lake during the men's fishing trip yesterday."

"Accidentally," my mom adds.

"Yes, accidentally," I clarify. "Because really he didn't want to push Grayson into the lake. He wanted to punch their dad in the face."

"Kinsley," my mom warns in a low voice.

I scoff, trying to muster a laugh that says *oh come on guys, it's fine* but instead, I sound manic. "Well, it's true."

"Why would your dad want to punch their dad?" Lena asks with a laugh. And bless her heart. She has no idea. She probably thinks the answer will be something funny, like a dispute over a beer koozie. Opposing football teams. Or maybe even which style of BBQ is supreme.

Now both Hazel and my mother look supremely uncomfortable about how to proceed. A heavy silence emerges as we all grapple with where to begin the story. Once again, this explanation is left up to me. And I'm drunk enough to go there.

"In a nutshell?" I begin, smoothing my hands over the satiny fabric of my wedding dress. "Because of some bullshit."

Hazel laughs nervously. I can tell my mom is gearing up to give her side of things.

"All we need to say—" Mom begins.

"Is that my mom hates Connor's mom because thirty-some years ago, my future mother-in-law tried to fleece my dad for money after claiming Dominic was a Cabana instead of a Daly."

Lena blinks rapidly, as though struggling to follow the circuitous path I laid out there. Hazel drags her middle finger back and forth over a brow. I just stare at all of them with a look that says *Am I wrong?*

"Kinsley, was that necessary?" Mom asks in a withering tone.

"She asked. I told her."

"I shouldn't have asked," Lena says. "I didn't realize—"

"You didn't know, and it's fine," I tell her. "I'm sick of this shit being buried and ignored. Do we have any more champagne?"

"Why don't you have a snack, Kins?" Hazel suggests.

"Yeah, I'm starving."

"I have sandwiches," Nancy offers suddenly, reminding me she's been here the whole time, quietly absorbing our drama. While she's gone in the back room, my mom is shaking her head, staring off into the distance.

"It's some Jerry Springer shit," I go on. "And you know what would be great? If they could get over it already."

Mom's outright glaring at me now, but her face softens when she turns to Lena and Hazel. "What Kinsley is trying to say is that it's just a very old wound that has never properly healed." To Hazel specifically, she says, "And as you can attest, it has never gotten in the way of our relationships with the rest of the Daly family members."

I scoff loudly. Drunkenly. "Oh, right. Like you guys are so warm with Connor." This is a truth-telling geyser now, a no-holds-barred confess-a-thon. I can't stop it. And I don't want to, either.

"Honey, we have done our best. There are plenty of families who would do far less and call it a day."

"Well that's not what Connor and I want for our lives. Two openly hostile sets of parents calling it their best effort." Now I'm feeling saucy but also sad. Nancy comes back out with a tray of tiny sandwiches, and I head toward her.

"Where's your restroom?"

"Back there, honey," she says, gesturing down the hallway she just came from. I scoop up three tiny sandwiches and follow to where she pointed. I gobble one sandwich down in front of the bathroom door, and my rumbling stomach reminds me how much I needed that. I stand there, shaking my head and chewing, before heading for the second sandwich. I don't even know what I'm eating—I'm just that level of starving where anything remotely nutritious tastes like the most amazing recipe ever. I inspect the last sandwich in my hand as I inhale the second one. Looks like sliced ham, white bread, and mustard. Genius. Somebody should call Gordon Ramsay and let him know about this amazing combination. I down the third with abandon.

After I've taken my time-out, I feel slightly recuperated. I never had to pee to begin with, I just needed to compose myself. So I return to the fitting area, feeling leveled out and more clear-headed.

As soon as I step toward the podium, my mom gasps so loud it sends a chill down my spine. She points to me, her eyes saucer-wide.

"Kinsley!"

Nancy mutters a swear word and darts away. Hazel clamps a hand over her mouth and Lena just watches me like she's seen a ghost.

"What is it?" I demand, twisting to find Nancy. "What happened?"

"You—you got—" Lena starts.

"Mustard! On your wedding dress!" Mom finishes.

The words don't entirely make sense. I look down at myself, and that's when I spot the stadium mustard–colored blob. My mouth parts yet I can't make a noise, though on the inside I'm screaming.

"I can fix this!" Nancy trills, rushing back out to the fitting area. "I have exactly what we need."

A high-pitched laugh rolls out of me. This is fine. Everything is fine. "Wow, that was an oopsie, huh?"

Nancy grimaces as she sets to work delicately wiping away the mustard, followed by spraying me down with something in an unlabeled bottle. "Quite an oopsie."

As I watch her work the stain over, all of the stress of the week descends upon me. And on top of it all? I just ruined my wedding dress.

A sob hitches in my throat, and then the tears come. I cover my face with my hands, feeling everything at once. Hopeless. Pathetic. Ridiculous. All the bad things, swirled into a melting sundae and poured over my head. My mom is at my side instantly.

"Honey," she begins, her tone firm and reassuring. "We will get this stain out. Look at how much Nancy has helped already."

"You won't be able to even see it after she's done," Hazel adds.

"I'm the expert, my dear, I promise!" Nancy quips as she keeps working amid the bride-to-be meltdown.

But it's not just the dress, though that is definitely the cherry on top of my melting, disgusting sundae. I just can't stop crying long enough to say that.

"Your wedding is going to be perfect, honey," my mom says, rubbing my back. "Nancy will fix this stain, and you will be the image of perfection on your big day."

I sniffle, finding a break in my tears to blurt out, "It will never be perfect."

"Honey, why would you say that?"

This isn't the champagne talking. This is the repressed stress of years of inter-family bitterness. The mounting tension of unresolved drama finally coming to a Vesuvius-style finale.

"How can it be perfect?" I ask her, wiping away some tears. "It's impossible when you hate my future husband, and my future mother-in-law hates me. And maybe you don't hate *him*, but you've hated his *family*, and that still hurts. Because they are good people, and *we* are good people. And we deserve to be together and happy. But this bullshit you guys bring along is only ever going to be a dark cloud over all of us. You guys think you can contain it and act like it stays on the sidelines, well...not anymore. Because I'm about to be a Daly, mom. And what then?" I toss my arms out to the side. Poor Nancy. I bet she never expected the level ten drama today. Hell, either did I.

"Honey, I have never hated Connor, and I promise you—" Mom begins softly.

"I'm not upset about the dress," I tell her. "Honestly, I could go get married in a mustard bottle, with my dress shredded by cougars, and I wouldn't even care. As long as these two families make the fuck up, I don't care. I will recite my vows draped in marshmallows if I have to."

"Atta girl," Lena says. "Marshmallows."

Once that's out of me, I take a cleansing breath. "Holy shit. Sorry Nancy. This got weird."

She smirks up at me, her eyes glinting with understanding. "My dear, that's not even close to the worst I've seen in here. And besides, you're fighting for family. That's not usually what starts the arguments in these parts."

However noble the fight feels, I still don't trust that I'll win in the end.

# CHAPTER SIX

CONNOR

"Ohhh, *finally*." Kinsley's appreciative sigh brings a smile to my face. She stretches out on the lounge chair, tucked between me and Lena on the deck of our rental house.

We have finally moved out of my parents' house and into our own wedding oasis. Lena sips happily on a margarita I made for the girls after dinner. I grab Kinsley's hand, bringing her knuckles to my lips.

"This is beautiful," Lena says. We're all facing the lake. Water laps at the rocky beach about twenty feet away, and sailboats dot the horizon like a painting. The temperature is still warm but bordering on chilly while the sky begins the burnt transition to dusk.

"This is Bayshore," I tell her. "Our lakeside Ohio oasis."

"I'd come here every year," Lena says. "In fact, maybe I could start tagging along on the yearly pilgrimage." She slurps loudly at her margarita. "You got any other brothers you don't know about that I could have?"

Kinsley snorts. "Who wants to place a bet that one of our fathers had a child out of wedlock and plans to blame it on the other family?"

Lena snickers. We've been rehashing all evening what went down inside Necessary Needles with Lena's colorful support of how Kinsley stood up for our happiness. Personally, I'm glad she had the meltdown and confronted her mother. Now if there were only a way to convince our stubborn parents to actually bury the hatchet.

"Well, if you *do* find a spare Daly brother, send him my way," Lena says. "Hell, I'll even take a Daly cousin."

"There's plenty of those," I tell her. "None quite as good looking, though."

As if on cue, Maverick pulls into the short driveway at the side of the rental house. His door slams a moment later, and then he's jogging toward the deck. When he shoots us all a big grin with a smooth "Hey, guys," Lena's brows immediately shoot to the sky.

"Maverick!" Kinsley pops out of her lounge chair and pulls him into a hug. "I've been wondering when you'd come around."

"Just got back from a gig in Cleveland," he says, settling onto an empty deck chair across from the three of us. He's dressed in a simple black T-shirt and black cargo pants, the sign he's come straight from the food truck. "Sorry if I smell like French fries."

Lena is blinking impatiently at us, as though encouraging the introductions.

"Lena, meet Maverick. This is Connor's youngest brother." Kinsley watches her friend as Maverick leans forward to shake her hand, and then adds, "and I'm sorry to say, he's taken."

"Dammit," Lena mutters. "Nice to meet you, Maverick."

Mavericks sends us a confused look. "What now?"

"Lena's looking for a spare Daly," I tell my brother. "But we've all been snapped up."

Maverick smiles, but it looks sad.

"You fixed things with Scarlett, right?" I ask him.

"Not yet." He clears his throat, suddenly very interested in the laces of his shoes. "I gotta figure out where her troupe is going next. And then I'm flying there to surprise her, wherever it is."

I can tell he's nervous about it. I reach out to squeeze his shoulder. "You got this, bro. You two love each other so much. You have for years."

He nods, running a hand through his dark locks. "You're right. I just wish Lettie could be here this weekend. I really wanted to bring her to your wedding—hell, and Dom's—but she's with the troupe, and I'm not gonna press it."

"You'll show her the pictures," Kinsley says, "and it will be glorious."

"Besides, the important thing is that the two of you don't miss your *own* wedding," I add. "And trust me, we will all be there when Mr. Playboy Daly ties the knot."

Maverick laughs. "You think we're gonna get married?"

"There's no other option for either of you," I tell him. "Have you ever actually looked at yourselves? I know I don't see you guys all the time, but I called it at Gray's wedding in the spring."

Maverick picks at a fingernail, a warm smile tugging at his lips as a lock of his hair dangles across his forehead.

"Yeah, that was pretty obvious," Kinsley adds. "I actually thought you two had come together until Connor told me halfway through the reception that you'd brought a different date."

I snort. "That poor girl."

"If you guys keep this up, you're going to force me to skip your wedding so I can go hunt Lettie down," Mav warns.

"And *this* is why I want a Daly man," Lena exclaims.

"Listen, you need something to drink," Kinsley says, clapping her hands together. "I'll go get you a margarita. What do you think?"

Mav agrees, and she heads into the kitchen. While she's inside, Mav leans forward. "Dude, what's this I hear about Kinsley's dad trying to drown Gray?"

"That story gets better the further away from the source it gets," Lena quips.

"He didn't try to drown him," I tell Mav. "But it was an insane morning. You should be glad you couldn't come. In fact—" I reach for my phone and swipe to the camera roll. "Let me show you the one piece of photographic evidence I have from the day. The first and probably last attempt at a Daly-Cabana peace accord."

Mav snickers as I scan the pictures. But something is off. I don't recognize any of these photos. Something white snags my attention and I enlarge the photo.

And then Kinsley in her wedding dress fills the screen.

My eyes go wide, drinking her in. I'm assaulted by conflicting emotions. *Holy shit she's so gorgeous* followed immediately by *I shouldn't be looking at this. What have I done?*

I turn the phone off and set it back on the arm rest where I found it. New phones: 5, Connor & Kinsley: 0.

"What's wrong?" Maverick asks.

"Nothing," I say, picking up the *other* phone that looks exactly like mine. I blink rapidly as I open my own camera roll. What do I do now? Admit the gaffe? Gush to Kinsley how she looks even more like an angel I don't deserve? My heart is pounding as I pull up the one photo Dom snagged from the fishing outing, and I show Maverick, who smiles and nods.

"Looks pretty fucking awkward," he confirms.

"Awkward doesn't cover it," I say, forcing a laugh. "Maybe it would if we only had to deal with the projectile puking."

Lena cackles. "I wish I could have been there."

Kinsley breezes out of the house a moment later, and the sight of her strawberry blonde beauty makes my throat tighten. This is my future wife. And that dress...holy shit that dress...

"Here you go, Mav." She hands him off a salt-rimmed margarita, then assesses our drinks. "Anybody need a refill?"

"I'm good for now," Lena says. I can't answer though, because I'm still overcome with emotion and confusion. Kinsley's brows draw together as her gaze lands on me.

"Connor? Are you okay?"

I nod, leaning back into my chair. "Yeah. Of course. Why wouldn't I be?" If she knew that I accidentally saw her wedding dress, it will be just one more thing on top of her shit pile. But how can I keep that from her? The conundrum forms a gridlock inside my body.

"I don't know. You look like you saw a ghost. Is our rental house haunted?"

"It's those Lake Erie perch ghosts," Maverick says grimly before he takes a sip of his drink.

"It...uh..." My gaze sweeps over her. I can't do anything but imagine the big day now. Standing in front of the lake with her, as we marry in the gazebo, surrounded by friends and family. This is what all our planning has led to. The past three years of happiness will finally culminate in marriage.

"Are you crying?" she asks softly.

I massage my forehead. "No, I'm just thinking about Saturday. How good it's gonna be." I take her hands in mine and bring them to my lips. "I just love you so much, Kinsley. I can't wait to marry you."

She grins, sinking back into her deck chair.

"*Definitely* need a Daly man," Lena says.

Kinsley reaches for her phone, swipes it open, and then freezes. She sends me a suspicious look, eyes narrowed, question marks forming in the air between us.

"Connor," she begins.

"I'll get refills," I offer. "In fact, I better just make a new batch. Your sisters will be here soon, after all."

"Weston and Nova should be heading over soon, too," Maverick says after checking his phone. "They landed in Cleveland about an hour ago."

"Yeah. See? More margs." I lean down to press a kiss to Kinsley's forehead, but she dodges me, eyes still narrowed accusingly.

"Did you look at my pictures?" she asks point-blank.

My limbs go warm and tingly. I can already feel my face betraying me—the honey-sweet adoration overcoming me, the way my heart is melting just from beholding her in the golden rays of sunset.

"Sunny-kins," I start, but I can't fight the enormous smile that takes over my face. Shit. I didn't expect to fall *more* in love with her just because of a dress. But it's not just the dress. It's the entire day. It's what it stands for: our commitment, our future, our happiness.

"I didn't mean to," I finally say, but I can't continue, because the smile won't let me. And then the laughter comes. This is awful. But it's so amazing.

Her mouth parts, both shock and amusement etching itself into her beautiful face. *The face of my wife.*

"You saw my wedding dress?" she screeches.

"I picked up my phone!" I blurt, pointing down at our phones, resting next to each other on the arm rest like a masochistic exercise in confusion. "But it was your phone. I wanted to show Maverick the picture from the boating trip—"

Kinsley covers her face with her hands and my stomach pitches to my feet. Both Lena and Mav are watching intently with grimaces on their faces. *Shit shit shit.* If I make her cry again, after the day she's had, I'll go find an *Eternal Sunshine* mind scrubbing procedure myself in advance of the wedding. But then I notice she's not crying. She's shaking. With laughter.

"Are you kidding me?" she says up toward the heavens, as though pleading with God himself.

"It was an honest mistake," I tell her, gathering her into my arms. "And babe. Babe. *Babe.*" I press my forehead to hers and speak quietly so only she can hear this. "I have never seen a more gorgeous sight in my life. And yes, I shed a tear. Because you are the woman of my dreams. You are everything I've ever wanted and so much more. Let's just call it our perfectly inappropriate good luck token in advance of the wedding."

She's shaking with silent laughter as she presses her lips to mine in a kiss. Then she cups my face in her hands, her periwinkle gaze searching my face.

"Honestly, I don't even care at this point," she says, sounding delirious. Or euphoric. Or maybe some new combination that only this wedding week could create. "My dad almost killed Gray—"

"That gets more dramatic every time for sure," Lena cracks.

"I spilled mustard on my wedding dress," Kinsley continues, "And now the groom has *seen the dress* two days before the wedding. Does anything matter anymore?"

My grin is ear-to-ear as I pull her tighter into my arms.

"I'll just be happy when this wedding is over," she confesses dreamily, stroking my cheek.

"Now that," I tell her, pressing my forehead to hers, "is the most romantic thing I've ever heard in my life."

# CHAPTER SEVEN

KINSLEY

Friday morning I'm awoken by Connor. Soft kisses to my spine. His thick arms wrapped around me. That delicious arousal pressed against my ass cheeks.

A smile drifts to my face, and I snuggle into him, wiggling my butt against him.

"You're awake," he murmurs, sinking his teeth into the side of my neck.

"Mmmm." My nipples go hard instantly. Desire pools in my core, still as strong as it was in the beginning. He palms my hip, digging his fingers into the flesh there.

"This is our last day to have sex out of wedlock," he reminds me. "We better take full advantage of it."

"Oh my god, you're right," I mumble, turning to face him. His blue eyes are sharp with desire. "After tomorrow, there will be no more immoral and adulterous behavior between us."

"Nope," he says, his hands making hot trails over my hips. One slips between my legs, beneath the fabric of my panties. "We're about to be legitimate. Law abiding. One hundred percent *married*."

I giggle as he buries his face in the hollow of my neck. He swipes his hot fingers back and forth over my mound, teasing me. Impatience swells in me—I am usually *the horniest* right after I wake up—and I push him onto his back, slipping on top of him.

"Ohh, Kins." He grabs at my ass cheeks, rooting me against him. My panties are damp already as our groins collide. We sleep in only our undies anymore, which leaves him free to run a hand up my waist before latching onto my breast. He tweaks a nipple as I rock back and forth on top of him. We are tuned in, connected, hopelessly in love. I grin down at him as our bodies follow the rhythm that only we know, that we have created with our love. He bites at his bottom lip, his gaze intense as he grinds the steel of his erection against me.

And then I'm up on my knees, pulling aside my panties while he works to free himself from the confines of his boxer briefs. His cock slides hot and hard against my slick folds, nudging and prodding my clit while I hover over him, desperate for him to line us up.

"Connor," I groan, while he teases me. "Please. I need it."

"I know you do," he grunts, bracing me at the hip while he runs his cockhead back and forth over my clit. "I need it too, babe."

And then he guides himself into place, his thickness pushing into me and I sink down, down around him. He stretches me as he always does, and the pleasure zips through me, hot and lurid, as though we haven't done this thousands of times before. My nipples are stiff peaks as I claim every inch of him, sinking down until there's nothing left for him to bury inside me.

His fingertips dig into the sides of my hips, mooring me as I rock against him. The feel of him filling me like this, so completely, always drives me to the edge extra fast. His eyes are heavy on me as I buck and grind, propping my palms against his chest as I drive myself higher and higher.

"Yesss, Kinsley," he groans, snaking a hand between my legs. He rubs at me while I ride him. Sparks fly, my core tightens, and it isn't long before I'm a whimpering, spasming mess on top of him. He grips my hips once I've fallen off the ride and keeps me moving against him, squeaking out the last dregs of my pleasure while he finds his own peak. His heat fills me, oozing out from between us, while we both pant to catch our breaths.

"That," he finally says after we've been locked in stupefied bliss, "was extra immoral and adulterous."

"I know it was," I finally whisper, leaning down to kiss him. "I love you so much, Connor."

He doesn't let me go immediately, coaxing a few more kisses out of me before allowing me to peel myself off him. We get ourselves cleaned up and ready for the day. This is a big one—though not quite as big as tomorrow, which is *the* day—and I want to be on my game. I've got a potential matriarch clash scheduled at eleven a.m. at the nail salon. My mom, sisters, Lena, Annette, and a few others have all been invited to attend. If we can get through that unscathed, then it only puts more pressure on the rehearsal tonight for things to unravel. And I'm not going to be the sad sack melting down after a glass and a half of champagne. Not again. Not until tomorrow, at least.

Connor is humming while he dresses. I pick out a pair of leggings and a flowy top, and then check in with my phone, only to realize it's Connor's.

"When are we going to get phone cases?" I demand, reaching for the one that is actually my phone.

"We could start by changing our backgrounds," he says from the bathroom.

"But I really like this picture as my background," I tell him.

"So do I."

I laugh to myself. This is where we always end up. "Okay, so how about this? I'll just put the picture of myself in the wedding dress as my lock screen so you can see it as many times as possible before our wedding day."

Water splashes, followed by a gargle. Then he says, "Serious? Because I'm not opposed to that. In fact, once we're married, that'll probably be my lock screen for the next year."

"We'll have better pictures after the wedding, you know. You won't need a photo from the day I got champagne drunk and let all our family skeletons out of the closet."

"I like that moment better for our family history," Connor says, coming out of the bathroom a moment later. "Besides, those skeletons are feisty. They've been cooped up in there too long. They needed some air."

"Well, let's just make sure they don't slink back into the closet," I tell him, wrapping my arms around his waist. "Now that they're out, I want to make sure they roam free. Make a name for themselves. Become gainfully employed and shit like that."

Connor strokes the side of my face. "Speaking of gainful employment...with all the drama of being home with family, I haven't had any time to stress about our business."

"Me neither."

"I guess we should thank our parents for that, at least." He presses a kiss to the tip of my nose.

"Yes. A feud so eternal and disruptive that we managed to forget entirely about our career." I look down at the phones, one of which is mine, though I can't tell right now. When I see the time, I sigh. "It's time to get this last full adulterous day started, babe. The mani-pedi starts soon, and then we've got the rehearsal. Do you think we'll make it out alive?"

"Probably," he says. "And if we don't, we've got a nice family of skeletons to live with in the closet."

# CHAPTER EIGHT



Time ticks onward, dragging me with it. I approach each new hour with cautious optimism, big smiles, and a healthy dose of suspicion. The matriarch mani-pedi comes and goes without incident, which feels like a Get Out of Jail Free card, only because Annette couldn't come and most of us ladies were separated throughout different parts of the nail salon during the prettifying routines.

And then the rehearsal happens. It is lively, beautiful, and fun, which only increases my suspicion. Sure, our sets of parents didn't glance at each other once through the practice runs and during the ensuing dinner, so that might have helped. But still, after a full twenty-four hours of absolutely zero drama, I'm starting to get a little worried...and even, dare I say it, excited for my own wedding.

Discounting the parental feud, everything has been going wonderfully, maroon van included. All of our loved ones are here. We've stayed on task, had multiple social events, and I managed to mostly not-ruin my wedding dress.

So when the morning of the wedding comes and I wake up slowly, smiling, stretching out in bed next to my almost-husband, I'm expecting some sort of relaxed jaunt through wedding day bliss. But what I actually receive is a sucker punch from the nuptial gnomes.

My sister Kestral is at the door of our rental at eight a.m., pounding like the house is on fire and we haven't been made aware. I stumble to greet her in a robe, and her big green eyes look at me in disbelief.

"Kinsley! We have to be at the hair salon in ten minutes!"

So that's how the day starts. I force myself into something resembling an outfit, Kestral pushes me into her car. I don't even get to say goodbye to Connor but, well, I guess I'll see him at the wedding. My mom and our other sister Katie are already at the salon when I get there, thumbing through magazines. From there, it's high-grade bridal party preparation. Lena shows up later for the professional makeup phase of the morning, blessedly bringing donuts and coffee, which I try to inhale around the application of makeup products I've never even heard of before, much less own. Apparently I've been contoured, which sounds painful until I look in the mirror and almost choke on my sprinkle donut.

It's me. Except, it's not. Or rather, it's the Kinsley Cabana-Soon-To-Be-Daly who has only ever existed in my imagination. I lower my donut, blinking at this rapturous creature in the reflection. My strawberry blonde hair is twisted into an elegant updo with soft waves framing my face. My complexion is perfect. My lips are huge and glossy. I am both powerful woman and gorgeous fairytale creature.

And then the tears start.

"Honey, no, don't cry," my makeup artist tuts. "I used waterproof mascara, but we want this to last *all day*."

"You are phenomenal at what you do," I tell her between sobs.

My sisters hug me from both sides while Lena plies me with another donut. But this time, I refuse. "I can't mess up my lipstick."

The makeup artist gives me a blast of setting spray, and then we're off. I check in with Connor, who's somehow drinking Bloody Marys with his brothers at the venue already. By this time we're ready for lunch, which means off to the venue. We selected an event space with floor-to-ceiling windows overlooking the lake with an attached brick-laid patio for the reception. Though the ceremony itself will be outside in the gazebo, set against a cluster of azaleas and roses mere feet from the lakeshore.

My sisters pick up and deliver lunch to the bridal dressing room, where I'm stowed away like a hostage. We feast on gourmet grilled cheese sandwiches—as delicately as possible—before it's time to get dressed. Lena, my sisters, and Hazel—London is resting with her feet up somewhere in the main hall—get themselves ready before they begin to fuss over me. I just sit back and enjoy it. My mom shows up in time to help me zip the wedding dress, and from then on she and I trade off shedding tears.

Because holy shit. Here we are. We made it to the wedding day.

Hazel helps me make sure we have everything in these final tense and dreamy moments before the bridesmaids are whisked away to take their places and the dash toward *I do* begins. Grammy Ethel's wedding rings? Connor has them. My vows? Tucked inside my bra. Garter belt? Awkwardly venturing toward my crotch.

A soft knock sounds on the outside of the door, and Lena gasps. "Is it time?"

Hazel whooshes toward the door in her floor-length buttercup-yellow gown. Because yes, our wedding colors are buttercup yellow, navy, and white. Connor insisted on the yellow—*"There's no other color that fits my sunflower, Sunny-kins."* You can't argue with a man in love.

When she pulls open the door, Annette Daly is waiting on the other side. She is the classic dark-haired beauty, her tresses pulled back into an elegant knot. Diamonds glint in her earlobes as she smiles nervously, peering inside.

"Hey, ladies. Can I come in and chat with the bride real quick?"

"Of course," I blurt, waving her in. Mom stiffens at my side, and the air grows noticeably tighter as Annette's gaze meets my mom's. Annette takes a moment to look me up and down, bringing her hands over her heart space.

"You look incredible, dear," she whispers. And that's when I notice tears shimmering in her eyes. "I just wanted to come sit down with you before everything got started."

"Yes, please. Join us." I gesture around, as though there's much to offer beyond curling irons and makeup boxes. Annette smiles past me at my sisters and Lena, who resume their own last-minute make-up touches in front of a big mirror on the far wall. Then her electric blue gaze settles on me, the eyes that all her sons inherited, and she draws a deep breath.

"I just wanted to come offer some wishes for your wedding," Annette says, smoothing the front of her dress. I've never seen her like this: nervous, maybe out of her element. Annette has always been the distant Daly matriarch who watched over her handsome sons with a quiet fierceness. But here, surrounded by women, I realize there's a side of Annette Daly that maybe I've never gotten to tap into. Not that she'd have let me tap into it, of course. But where my father was the lone male in a sea of women, Annette's life has been the beautiful woman, surrounded by devastatingly handsome men.

"You have been a steady fixture in my son's life," Annette says slowly, focusing her intense gaze on me. "You inspire him. It's plain to see. You two lead a beautiful, admirable life. The type of life that I respect and envy." Annette squeezes my arm before continuing.

"All I've ever wanted was for my sons to be loved for the incredible, dynamic men they are. And you don't just love Connor for those things. You help him elevate those qualities."

Tears return to my eyes. I wish I could be recording this for posterity, but I forget where I put my phone. Connor probably picked it up accidentally somewhere.

"So you, Kinsley, have helped me achieve one of my greatest dreams: to see my boy become the best version of himself I could have hoped for. Thank you for that. Sincerely."

I reach for a tissue, dabbing at the corner of my eye. "You're welcome. I just...I don't know what to say."

"You don't have to say anything, honey. I just wanted to thank you for loving Connor the way he deserves to be loved." She reaches for my hands, giving one a squeeze. "I know things weren't easy in the beginning. And I'm sorry that so much of our historical...*shit*...made its way into the present."

My mom straightens her back. She's been keeping watch nearby while pretending to arrange an open makeup box. "Mm-hmm."

Annette glances at my mom, then looks at me once more. "I'm excited to have you enter the family. To carry the Daly name. And I will treat you as my own daughter."

Her words warm my heart, but Mom has other plans.

"Hopefully that doesn't mean blaming her for things she didn't do," Moms mutters.

Annette's sharp gaze lands on my mom. "Excuse me?"

"I wasn't even in your house an hour before you declared I broke a glass deliberately," Mom says. "I'm not sure why I should believe my daughter will fare much better."

All the warmth that Annette's words had conjured begins to fade away.

"It won't be hard for her to be better than you," Annette says in a controlled but threatening tone. "Since I won't have to rely on her for moral support, only to have her turn her back on me."

"Or do you plan to continue punishing her for something you think I did?" Mom asks.

I blink rapidly, looking between the two beautiful women. I can't believe they used to be best friends. And now here we are. Still caught in a snit from the eighties.

Before Annette can respond—and I can tell she's got a doozy brewing from the way her lip curls—I hurry to say, "Uh, ladies? Time out?" I make a T with my hands. "I'm not sure if you've noticed, but I've been doing my part to get you two to get fuck the over this. Not just you two—the four of you, actually. So either we're going to get to the bottom of this right now, once and for all, or we're going to leave it in the rearview mirror forever." I pause, feeling so powerful in this moment. For good measure, I add, "Or else."

"We used to be close," Annette tells me sadly. "But after I broke up with your father, he and Lisa started getting closer. I was okay with it."

"It seemed like it at first," Mom says softly.

"I was okay with it in the beginning," Annette adds. "Until that horrible party at Jackson's." To me, Annette says, "I was dating Damon at the time, but Jack and I were friendly. We ended up at the same party one night, but we all drank way too much. I passed out, and when I came to, I was in bed beside your father—"

"Oh, there's this story again," Mom groans.

Annette's throat bobs, and she takes a moment. "It hurts when your best friend won't even listen when you try to tell her about a frightening time in my life. That's when you stop being best friends."

"No, we stopped being best friends when you tried to pin an unplanned pregnancy on Jack," Mom says. "You know nothing happened that night with Jack. Or Dominic would have grown up spending holidays and every other weekend at our house." To me, Mom adds, "She got knocked up the old-fashioned way by her boyfriend, and tried to blame your father, who did nothing wrong."

Annette's nostrils flare. "I found out I was pregnant a month later. All I could think about was that night at the party." Sadness fills Annette's face. "I was pregnant, scared, and my best friend walked away from me."

My head is spinning. This isn't just some old drama. This is a heart-wrenching story that I absolutely cannot participate in right now.

Hazel raps softly on the door. I hadn't even realized she'd stepped out. "Ladies. They're ready."

Annette clutches my hands. "I didn't want for this to come up. I just wanted to say thank you...and I wish the absolute best for both of you." She offers a small smile before hurrying out of the room. I twist to look at Mom.

"Really? You ditched Annette when she got pregnant?"

"She lied about who the father was and threatened to take your father to court."

I heave a huge sigh. How much did any of that matter? It was over thirty years ago. And looking ahead...I could only see one clear path.

"I saw a woman who came here to open a door to the future," I tell my mom. "And that's where I'm heading. Where are you planning to go?"

Mom works on arranging my veil and says nothing. Lena and my sisters hurry out the door, where Hazel is waiting with a big smile.

"It's time."

# CHAPTER NINE

CONNOR

"Hey, you okay?"

Dom's rumbling question at my side reminds me that I've taken approximately fifteen deep breaths in the past minute. I probably sound like I'm close to hyperventilating, and it is his oath-bound duty to help me.

"Yeah. Yeah. I'm fine." I nod firmly as Dom squeezes my shoulder. "Just so fucking ready to get married."

Dom's broad smile calms me. Behind him, the rest of my brothers are lined up: Grayson winking over at Hazel on the bridesmaid side, Weston smiling out at Nova in the second row, and Maverick squinting off into the distance, probably trying to communicate telepathically with Scarlett. In front of us, rows and rows of white folding chairs spread out, all of them occupied by our guests. A buttercup-yellow path runs down the center aisle. All the bridesmaids have gathered on the other side of the yellow aisle, and while the three violinists at the back of the gathering switch to Pachelbel's

Canon in D, I could projectile puke all over again with how anxious and excited I am to see my almost-wife.

It doesn't matter that I saw her in the dress. I haven't seen her *today*, and every cell in my body is on the verge of revolting if I do not get her in my sight in the next thirty seconds.

"He's gonna pass out," Grayson murmurs from further down the line.

"You're one to talk," I shoot back.

"It's a known defect!" Gray says. "We Daly men can't handle the wedding wait." And he's not wrong. Both he and Dom were in very similar positions at different points this year, and I won't be surprised if we watch Weston and Maverick fall into the same boat soon enough.

Suddenly, Jack Cabana rounds the corner. I can see Kinsley's arm, and nothing more. My organs begin to dissolve. Everyone whooshes to standing, and I feel like I might actually crumple to the ground. Kinsley emerges from behind the corner next. My heart stops beating. Dom's hand is on my shoulder, the only thing reminding me I have a body, as I absorb this gorgeous woman.

The picture didn't do her justice. She is radiance and purity and endless smiles and every bit of everything I've ever loved about her. I would run down the aisle just so I could touch her sooner if I could remember how to use my legs.

"He's crying," Grayson tells Weston and Maverick.

I am. The tears have been in hiding for a week. I wipe at a cheek as Kinsley floats down the aisle toward me, the netted veil covering the ear-to-ear grin she wears. When she glides to a stop in front of me, she hugs her father. He flips the veil for her, and then she steps up to me. I grab her by the hips.

"No touching the bride yet," the minister says before clearing his throat.

"Sorry," I say, palms up. "Got a little excited."

Kinsley shakes with laughter, wiping at her eyes already. I take a moment to look her over as everyone in the audience takes their seats. Everything around us—the low rush of the lake churning against the rocky shore, the hundreds of people in attendance, the brilliantly crisp and perfect September day—all fades away as I behold her. I have never seen a more beautiful sight. My gaze falls on a little pin above her right breast. It says, "I'm the bride."

I jerk my chin toward her chest. "Did you think I'd forget?"

She shakes with more laughter, pressing a hand to her chest. "We couldn't get the mustard stain out entirely. This was Plan B."

Another round of laughter and tears overcomes her, which triggers my own. The ceremony hasn't even started yet and we're a mess.

The ceremony turns into a dreamy film reel from there. I'm both tuned in and drifting above the clouds as the minister reads through the ceremony. We light the unity candle—barely, given the lake breeze—and recite our vows. When Kinsley reaches the part about loving me forever at 3500 megahertz, my tears turn to laughter because at that same moment, a seagull uprising takes place not far from the shore. They are fighting over something, and the squalling is distracting. Uproarious. Kinsley dissolves in the middle of her vows, and I gather her into my arms where we laugh and laugh and laugh. And only we know why.

And then, the most important words come. "I now pronounce you husband and wife."

The minister gestures at us, and we take our cue. I cup Kinsley's face in my hands and kiss my sunbeam so hard that time seems to shudder to a stop. All I can sense is her brightness, her love, her warmth. When we break apart, we're both crying again.

"Thank you for giving us a chance three years ago," I tell her. "Even though I didn't deserve it."

"You're lucky you're impossible to resist," she says, wiping tears from her eyes. I take her hand and we face the crowd, bringing our hands into the air. Everyone cheers as we make our way down the aisle. We head to the edge of the flower-lined patio, where we can greet everyone before reporting for pictures. My brothers bounce down the middle aisle, waving at people in the audience like they're celebrities. The bridesmaids follow, London waddling last in line. Kinsley nudges me a moment later.

"Does London look okay to you?"

I watch her as she slowly takes her place at the end of the line. She's outrageously pregnant in her buttercup gown, which is pretty much all I notice. "Yeah, why wouldn't she?"

"Don't you think she looks...woozy, or something?"

"I mean, she's ready to pop sometime in the next two weeks, babe," I remind her. "I think 'woozy' is her natural state now."

"Right, but..." Kinsley shakes her head, eyes on her new sister-in-law. She pokes her head out of line to call for Dom's attention. "Dom! Does your wife need to sit down?"

Dom peers down the line. "London! Do you want to sit down?"

"Why would I want to sit down?" she calls out, cocking a hip, her yellow and white bouquet looking like it might double as a weapon if Dom's not careful.

"You've been on your feet for a while," Dom tells her.

London lets out an exaggerated sigh. "Dominic Daly, I can stand on my own two feet for more than a half hour, thankyouverymuch."

Dom sends Kinsley a smirk. "We tried."

The violin trio plays a rendition of Louis Armstrong's "What a Wonderful World" while our guests file out row by row to greet us. The early afternoon kisses us, the puffy autumn clouds the perfect backdrop as we shake hands, share greetings, give hugs. Once our guest-greeting duties are over and the guests have been herded into the reception hall for appetizers and music, the photographer signals for us. It's bridal party picture time.

Kinsley and I walk hand in hand to a manicured lawn adorned with weeping willows and daisies, inlaid with decorative rocks. The lake peeks through behind us, and we begin the photo shoot.

The photographer wants all of us lined up to start, but as we're getting into line, Dom and London are quietly discussing something off to the side.

"Hurry it up, Dalys!" I call out to them.

London looks exasperated as she joins the line. Dom jogs to his open spot on the groomsmen side, his jaw flexing.

"Everything okay, brother?" I ask him.

"She looks pale," he says. "But she won't hear it."

"I do not look pale," London objects from down the line. I stifle a laugh. "Note to self: marrying a doctor is not all fun and free blood pressure checks."

Laughter rolls through the bridal party. Dom shakes his head, tongue pressed into his cheek.

"That was a good one," I tell him.

"Oh, I know," he says, looking like he's fighting a smile. "I know."

The photographer gets to work snapping pictures. Kinsley and I morph through various stages of embracing and blissed out smiles. We do groomsmen and groom only next, followed by Kinsley and bridesmaids only. While my brothers and I are gathered behind the photographer, adding extra moral support and distraction to the ladies while they suffer through the endless clicking and posture adjustments, London cries out.

But her gasp lands more like a gunshot. Her mouth parts and her hands go to the front of her dress. Everyone looks at her in confusion.

"Holy shit, my water just broke!" she cries out.

# CHAPTER TEN

KINSLEY

*Her water broke. Her water broke.*

I'm watching dumbfounded for a few moments, and I struggle to process what's actually happening. Dom is off like a lightning bolt to London's side. He gathers her against him, neck bent as he talks quietly to her. She's nodding at whatever Dom tells her. Connor and the rest of the brothers are watching them with the same mouth-agape expression that betrays what we're all thinking:

*What the fuck now?*

"Ummmm," I begin unhelpfully, looking around. "Should we call a doctor?" It hits me a second later that Dom *is* a doctor, which Hazel quietly reminds me of around laughter. Lena and my sisters are gathered nervously behind London and Dom, looking as confused as the rest of us. I go to London's side, where she's got Dom's forearm in a death grip.

"Guys, what can I do?" I ask.

"Ohhhh, Kinsley," London moans, covering her face with her hands. "I'm so sorry. I'm so, so sorry."

"What are you sorry for?" I ask.

She gestures vaguely at her dress. "For all this!"

"London, this is fine. This is *exciting*," I tell her.

"I just didn't think it would happen now," she goes on, pressing a hand to her forehead. "My due date isn't for two more weeks."

"Babies come when they want," I tell London, gently squeezing her shoulder. "Even in the middle of a photo shoot."

"Are you sure you aren't upset?" she asks me. "I don't want to ruin your day. This is *your* day."

I can't help but laugh. "Ruin my day? London, this is making my day even better! Now will you go please have this baby?"

Dom sends me a grateful look and helps her hobble toward the reception hall. They're feet away from the door when my mom shoots outside, eyes wild. She gestures inside, urging Dom and London to follow her. Through the big windows, I watch my mom lead London to a tucked away portion of the hall, where she kneels in front of London. It looks like she's coaching her. Dom stands with his arms crossed behind her, nodding, looked stressed as hell.

But they've got this. Between Dom's medical license and my mom's experience in the labor and delivery ward, I'm pretty sure London could safely have the baby during the toast, and everything would be just fine.

"Do we need to call an ambulance or something?" Connor asks.

"Mom and Dom are on it," I tell him, pointing to where they're gathered behind the window. "The experts are in the house."

Collectively we watch what's going on for a few more moments before the photographer urges us to finish the photo session, sans Dom and London. We rearrange ourselves, hamming and giggling and alternating between holding me up and holding Connor up. Maverick scales Connor's shoulders at one point, and the two wobble around the manicured lawns, bursting with laughter, until Maverick finally slides back to earth.

When we've wrapped up pictures, the bridal party heads inside, leaving Connor and me alone on the lakeshore.

"So," Connor says, wrapping his arm around my waist as we look out at the whitecaps and the drifting gulls. "You think London's baby is gonna share our anniversary?"

"I hope so, even though London seemed mortified that it's taking away from our day."

"It would make it easier to remember our niece's birthday," Connor says.

"Yes, there's that."

A shout from the reception hall grabs our attention. Grayson is waving us over, whistling. Connor and I hurry toward the building as fast as my satin train and peep-toe flats will let me. When we get to the hall, forgoing the illustrious introduction of the new couple, the entire place is buzzing.

"Uh, apparently, London is progressing really fast," Grayson says, a confused look on his face. "I don't exactly know what that means, but—"

"Holy shit," I say as we round the corner to the secluded area where London is seated. She's clutching at her stomach, face contorted in pain. Annette is pacing nearby, looking worried. My mom is kneeling in front of London, rubbing her knees, repeating, "the baby isn't going to fall out. I promise you."

Dom is gnawing on the inside of his cheek, one hand pressed to his forehead.

"Is everything okay?" I ask him.

"Yeah. Your mom just checked her. She's at eight centimeters."

He must have noticed my dumbstruck face, because a grin erupts on his face. "It means we're close. And we need to leave. We're waiting on the ambulance now."

"Oh my God!" My eyes go wide, and I rush over to London's side. "London! This is so exciting!"

"Ohhhh my Godddd, Kinsleeey," she moans, resting her face against my arm. "I'm so sorry!"

"London, please," I tell her. "This is a magical occurrence. You're going to be a mommy!"

A smile drifts over her face, then her brows draw together and she goes silent. A moment later she lets out a whoosh of air. "Sorry. Contraction. Holy shit those assholes hurt."

"She's doing a great job," my mom says, using her calm-yet-firm labor & delivery voice. "I think she was progressing the entire wedding and she didn't even know it. Lucky girl."

"Yeah, lucky," London says, her voice watery, then her brows pinch together again. "Ohhh, here comes another asshole."

"You're doing so good," I tell London. "You couldn't have done it better. You witnessed the wedding *and* you're bringing new life into the world. This is the definition of multi-tasking. You're a rock star, London."

She laughs, reaching for my hand, but the squeeze turns into a vice grip as her eyebrows tell me another contraction is wringing her out.

"Ambulance is here!" Weston calls out.

Dom, my mom, Annette, and I all help London waddle to the back door where the squad is wheeling a gurney toward the building along a cement sidewalk lined with rose bushes. London meets them at the door, waves off their attempts to help, hauls her butt up on the stretcher, and collapses backward gratefully. Dom gives my mother and his own each a big hug before trailing beside the gurney, hand clasped with London's. We all form a line along the windows, watching them load London inside and drive away.

"She's gonna do great," my mom says once we've all peeled our-selves from the windows. "I wasn't just saying that." To Annette, my mom adds, "You're about to be a grandmother."

Annette bursts into tears and wraps her arms around my mom. I can tell my eyes are wide as saucers as the two women hug and hug and hug.

I try not to look as stunned as I feel. Connor and I wander away to rejoin the reception, where we're promptly swallowed into a round of cheers and applause—the greeting we missed by hurrying in the side door. Music swells and dinner is served. Our bridal party makes sometimes heartfelt and sometimes silly toasts. Everyone is beaming and happy around us.

But the real stars of the show are our parents. Once the dance floor opens and everyone is fed, loose, and happy, I spot our fathers deep in conversation at one of the dinner tables. Our mothers are seated next to them, holding wine glasses and chatting enthusiastically. I have to blink about a hundred times to make sure I'm seeing this correctly.

Helping a son's wife in an unexpected birth moment is cause for a single hug between frosty ex-friends. But this?

This looks like two sets of adults hanging out and getting to know each other just for the hell of it.

Connor rubs my back. "Why are you crying again, babe? You getting the post-wedding sads?"

"Oh, I'm not sad, honey," I tell him, wrapping my arms around his waist. He is my rock, my light, and now, my husband. "I'm just the opposite. I'm happier than I've ever been in my life."

My mother's laughter pierces the air, and I gesture toward the Daly-Cabana reunion taking place in front of us. "Look. They could start a band with how well they're getting along right now."

"I think your dad would play the tuba," Connor states.

"Your dad would be on drums." We hash out the instrument choices for a few moments before deciding their band name would be Cabalys and kiss to seal this good fortune.

Because this hasn't just been our wedding day.

This has been a day of union. Of new beginnings. Of wild, exuberant happiness that can only serve as the benchmark for the rest of our lives.

And finally...*finally*...both of our families are here beside us. Ready for the ride.

# EPILOGUE

CONNOR

*Bzz. Bzz.*

"Let me guess," Kinsley says from across the kitchen of our rental house. We're back in Bayshore at the same rental house after our Aruba and Dominican Republic honeymoon, excessively tanned and lighter than clouds. She looks over at me with a dreamy smile. "It's Dom."

My brother has been texting nonstop with photos of the newest addition to the Daly family: *Charlotte Rose.* I grab for my phone, which I'm confident is my own after the lock screen flashes with Kinsley's fitting room photo, and nod.

"Oh yeah. New pictures."

Kinsley abandons the limes she was cutting and comes immediately to my side. A picture of the wispy-haired three-week-old fills our screen. She's grimacing over Dom's shoulder, where a long trail of spit-up cascades down the back of his button-up.

*DOM: #Dadlife.*

CONNOR: *Looks good on you, bro.*

Kinsley kisses my cheek before returning to her lime slicing duties. A burst of laughter from the patio grabs our attention and we both turn to look.

It's our parents, seated around the small, contained firepit in the backyard, roaring with laughter about something that is probably only funny to them.

"You know, I thought reconciliation was too much to hope for," Kinsley says, shaking her head as she pushes the limes into a serving bowl. "But this is crazier than that, even. They skipped over reconciliation and went straight to inside jokes and the cool-kids club."

"Swear to God, I tried to make a date with my mom tomorrow for lunch and she said she couldn't—*because of Lisa,*" I tell Kinsley.

She laughs. "I can't say I mind." I grab a pack of beers before we head outside with replenishments for our evening around the fire. Once we step onto the deck, the full force of our parent's conversation reaches us. My mom is shrieking with laughter about something while Lisa swats at her husband's chest. Dad is wiping at his eyes like he just laughed himself to tears. Kinsley and I share a look.

"Think they even noticed we left?" I joke.

"It's better they don't," she says, knocking me with her hip before heading down onto the grass. "That way, we can slip away later for more honeymoon sex."

I grin and follow her, my eyes glues to her lean, sun-kissed figure. Her hair is bleached out from our sunbathing marathon in Aruba. It was hard not to spend every second on the beach, especially when Weston and Nova live on it. Nova even talked Kinsley into a morning boudoir session, just the two of them, which Kinsley refuses to show me the pictures from just yet because of a secret something she has planned for me that she promises involves "ample underwear."

"Parents," Kinsley announces over the din. "We have returned."

"Hi, honey," Lisa says distractedly, before returning to the lively conversations happening between the of four of them. We share a knowing grin. A few empty chairs complete the big circle around the fire pit. We're waiting on Hazel and Gray still, who were both working late tonight, and Maverick, who promised he'd stop over one last time. He recently returned from Austin, where he "made up to Lettie for being the biggest dick in the world."

Truthfully, I'm relieved we scheduled this last stop in Bayshore before heading back to San Diego in a couple days. Now that we've taken a break from the business, Kinsley and I feel regenerated. Ready to tackle new challenges. Completely refreshed and creatively recharged.

Of course, the insane amounts of sex we had probably helped with that too.

I queue up my laptop, which sits on a small table next to me, where the plan is to show off the wedding photos that came in yesterday. They're downloading to my previewer while our parents chatter excitedly and Kinsley pours herself a margarita. Bulbous clouds hang low in the sky, steel gray floating against the cobalt hue of the impending night. The air is chillier now—it's almost October in Ohio—and Kinsley reaches for the cardigan she brought out.

"I love fall nights in Ohio," she coos.

"I love sharing fall nights in Ohio with you," I tell her, leaning over our chairs to press a soft kiss to her lips. My laptop makes a *whoosh* noise, which means the photos are ready.

"Parents and progenitors," I call out over the din. "The wedding photos are ready." It takes a few tries, but they calm down and finally focus on us. The four of them are flushed and beaming. Reconciliation looks good on them.

I position my computer so that everyone can see, and we begin cycling through the photos. It is a joyous, beautiful walk down memory lane. Kinsley keeps her hand clasped over her mouth, eyes shimmering, as the photos progress: the bridal party getting ready, the venue, the moment Kinsley and her father paused at the head of the aisle. The photographer even caught me in that raw, vulnerable state when I first laid eyes on Kinsley, which makes my mom say, "Oh, honey, will you look at that man in love?"

But the photos that elicit the biggest response are the group photos. Because unbeknownst to us, our photographer managed to capture the exact moment when London's water broke. The progression of photos is stunning. Hilarious, even. We flip through them sequentially a few times, watching her eyes round in the first picture, followed by her mouth turning into an O in the next photo, followed by her hands clutching the front of her dress. The next photo shows Dom mid-gallop on his way to attend to her.

"We need to print these for London and make sure she includes them in the baby book," Kinsley says after we've run through the progression a few more times.

"She can make a flip book," I suggest.

The photos cycle on but Kinsley and I just get lost in each other's gaze. Dusk falls dewy and cool around us while the fire keeps us warm.

But not quite as warm as the satisfaction humming in the air right now, the brazen contentment that crackles and ripples through us endlessly. Our parents shriek and laugh in the background while Kinsley and I speak volumes without uttering a single word.

This. Right here.

This is what we've been striving for. Not just good, but great. Two families at peace. My brothers in love. Our present days bright, but our futures brighter. These photos are just a small fraction of the memories that Kinsley and I have been creating together. Because now, all of our families are in the mix, happy and looking toward the horizon.

And if there's anything that will keep a smile on my face, it's that.

## THE END

*This might mark the end of the Bayshore series, but there's plenty more ahead! Want to get to know a new group of brothers? Meet the Fairchilds in The Bad Boys of Wall Street, my steamy billionaire romance series that starts with THE PRICE OF REVENGE (http://bo oks2read.com/price-of-revenge). This book follows Axel & Cora's SIZZLING second chance, enemies-to-lovers romance as they are forced to do business together 8 years after their messy breakup.*

*Looking for more small-town vibes? Check out Winter Harbor, my co-written series with Whitley Cox, which also follows a group of brothers: THE BASTARD HEIR (Winter Harbor #1) (http://books 2read.com/the-bastard-heir).*

Stay connected with me via my newsletter (http://bit.ly/EL-news letter), where I share teasers, sales, and other exciting news. Because BIG things are coming, friends!

Or join my reader group, EMBER LEIGH'S BLOSSOMS on Facebook, to hang out up-close and personal! Early looks at new covers, exclusive access to ARC sign-ups, and more.

Find me on...

FACEBOOK

INSTAGRAM

GOODREADS

BOOKBUB

http://www.emberleighromance.com/

***And before you go...***
Please consider leaving an honest review about this book! Even just a few words or a line mean so much to us authors.

# ALSO BY EMBER LEIGH

**THE BAD BOYS OF WALL STREET**
The Price of Revenge
The Price of Passion
The Price of Infamy
The Price of Forever

**WINTER HARBOR**
**(co-written with Whitley Cox)**
The Bastard Heir
The Asshole Heir
The Rebel Heir
The Matchmaking Heirs

**THE BAYSHORE SERIES**
Make Me Lose
Make Me Fall
Make Me Yours
Make Me Choose
Make Me Hot

Make Me Smile

**THE BREAKING SERIES**
Breaking the Rules
Changing the Game
Breaking the Sinner
Breaking the Habit
Breaking the Fall